New York T[...]*uthor*

"Brenda Jackson w[...]es
and characters you fall in love with."
—*New York Times* and *USA TODAY* bestselling author
Lori Foster

"Jackson's trademark ability to weave
multiple characters and side stories together
makes shocking truths all the more exciting."
—*Publishers Weekly*

"There is no getting away from the sex appeal and
charm of Jackson's Westmoreland family."
—*RT Book Reviews* on *Feeling the Heat*

"Jackson's characters are wonderful, strong,
colorful and hot enough to burn the pages."
—*RT Book Reviews* on *Westmoreland's Way*

"The kind of sizzling, heart-tugging story
Brenda Jackson is famous for."
—*RT Book Reviews* on *Spencer's Forbidden Passion*

"This is entertainment at its best."
—*RT Book Reviews* on *Star of His Heart*

* * *

Stern is part of The Westmorelands series:
A family bound by loyalty...and love!
Only from *New York Times* bestselling author
Brenda Jackson and Harlequin Desire!

* * *

If you're on Twitter,
tell us what you think of Harlequin Desire!
#harlequindesire

Dear Reader,

I love writing about the Westmorelands because they exemplify what a strong family is all about, mainly the sharing of love and support. For that reason, when I was given the chance to present them in a trilogy, I was excited and ready to dive into the lives of Zane, Canyon and Stern Westmoreland.

It is hard to believe that Stern is my twenty-sixth Westmoreland novel. It seemed like it was only yesterday when I introduced you to Delaney and her five brothers. I knew by the time I wrote Thorn's story that I just had to tell you about their cousins who were spread out over Montana, Texas, California and Colorado.

It has been an adventure and I enjoyed sharing it with you. I've gotten your emails and snail mails letting me know how much you adore those Westmoreland men, and I appreciate hearing from you. Each Westmoreland—male or female—is unique and the way love conquers their hearts is heartwarming, breathtaking and totally satisfying.

I love writing stories where best friends fall in love. In this story, Stern and JoJo are best friends who understand each other and want the best for each other. I enjoyed how they finally realize their relationship is based on more than a close friendship—it is grounded in true love.

I hope you enjoy this story about Stern and JoJo.

Happy reading!

Brenda Jackson

BRENDA JACKSON

Stern

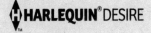
HARLEQUIN® DESIRE

To my husband,
the love of my life and my best friend, Gerald Jackson, Sr.

Happy birthday to all the members of the 1971 Class of
William Raines High School in Jacksonville, Florida. You know
what milestone we hit this year and we are still the greatest. Ichiban!

To my good friend Linda Reagor.
Thanks for the hunting lesson. I appreciate you!

Greater love hath no man than this,
that a man lay down his life for his friends.
—*John* 15:13

ISBN-13: 978-0-373-73264-7

STERN

Copyright © 2013 by Brenda Streater Jackson

Recycling programs
for this product may
not exist in your area.

Printed in U.S.A.

www.Harlequin.com

Books by Brenda Jackson

Harlequin Desire

Silhouette Desire

Harlequin Kimani Arabesque

Harlequin Kimani Romance

*The Westmorelands
ΔMadaris Family Saga
ΩSteele Family titles

Other titles by this author
are available in ebook format.

BRENDA JACKSON

is a die "heart" romantic who married her childhood sweetheart and still proudly wears the "going steady" ring he gave her when she was fifteen. Because she believes in the power of love, Brenda's stories always have happy endings. In her real-life love story, Brenda and her husband of more than forty years live in Jacksonville, Florida, and have two sons.

A *New York Times* bestselling author of more than seventy-five romance titles, Brenda is a recent retiree who now divides her time between family, writing and traveling with Gerald. You may write Brenda at P.O. Box 28267, Jacksonville, Florida 32226, email her at WriterBJackson@aol.com or visit her website at www.brendajackson.net.

THE DENVER WESTMORELAND FAMILY TREE

Raphel and Gemma Westmoreland

Stern Westmoreland (Paula Bailey)

Adam (Clarisse) Thomas (Susan)

Dillon (Pamela) ①   Micah (Kalina) ⑥   Jason (Bella) ⑤   Riley (Alpha) ⑧   Canyon (Keisha) ⑩   Stern (JoJo) ⑪   Brisbane   Aidan   Bailey

Ramsey (Chloe) ②   Zane (Channing) ⑨   Derringer (Lucia) ④   Megan (Rico) ⑦   Gemma (Callum) ③   Adrian

⑪ Stern

① Westmoreland's Way
② Hot Westmoreland Nights
③ What a Westmoreland Wants
④ A Wife for a Westmoreland
⑤ The Proposal
⑥ Feeling the Heat
⑦ Texas Wild
⑧ One Winter's Night
⑨ Zane
⑩ Canyon

One

"Stern, what can a woman do to make a man want her?"

Stern Westmoreland, who had been looking through the scope of his hunting rifle, jerked his head around at the unexpected question, nearly knocking the cap off his head.

He glared at the woman beside him who was staring through the scope of her own rifle. When a shot rang out, expletives flowed from his lips. "Dammit, JoJo, you did that on purpose. You asked me that just to ruin my concentration."

She lowered her rifle and frowned at him. "I did not. I asked you because I really want to know. And if it makes you feel better, I missed my target just now."

Stern rolled his eyes. So what if she had missed her shot *now?* Nothing had stopped her from taking down that huge elk yesterday when he had yet to hit anything, not even a coyote. On days like this he wondered why he always invited his best friend on these hunting trips. She showed him up each and every time.

Lifting his rifle and looking through the scope again,

he drew in a deep breath. He knew why he always invited JoJo. He liked having her around. When he was with her he could be himself and not a man trying to impress anyone. Their comfortable relationship was why she'd been his best friend for years.

"Well?"

He lowered the scope from his eye to look at her. "Well what?"

"You didn't answer me. What can a woman do to make a man want her? Other than jump into bed. I'm not into casual sex."

He couldn't help but chuckle. "I'm glad to hear that."

"What do you find funny, Stern? It's okay for *you* to be into casual sex but not *me?*"

Stern stared at her in astonishment. "What in the heck is wrong with you today? You've never been into drama."

JoJo's expression filled with anger and frustration. "You don't understand, and you used to understand me even when nobody else did." Without saying anything else she turned and walked off.

He watched her leave. *What the hell?* JoJo was being temperamental, and in all the years he'd known her she'd *never* been temperamental. What in the world was going on with her?

Deciding he wasn't in the mood to hunt anymore today, he followed JoJo down the path that led back to his hunting lodge.

After a quick shower, Jovonnie Jones grabbed a beer out of the refrigerator, pulled the tab and took a refreshing sip. She needed that, she thought as she left the kitchen to sit outside on the wooden deck and enjoy the picturesque view of the Rocky Mountains.

A few years ago Stern had stumbled on this lodge,

an old, dilapidated place that sat on more than a hundred acres of the best hunting land anywhere. In only two years, with the help of his brothers and cousins, the building had been transformed into one of beauty. It was a perfect hunting getaway. It offered black bears, deer, fox and other wildlife, but this was mainly elk country.

The lodge had been a good investment for Stern. When he wasn't using it, he leased it. It was a huge two-story structure with eight bedrooms, four full bathrooms and wooden decks that wrapped all the way around the house on both the first and the second floors. The common area included a huge kitchen and dining area and a sitting room with a massive brick fireplace. Plenty of floor-to-ceiling windows provided breathtaking views of the Rockies from every room.

She eased down in one of the outdoor cedar rocking chairs. Even after her hot shower and cold beer, she was still feeling frustrated and angry. Why couldn't Stern take her seriously and answer her question? It should work in her favor that she was best friends with a man most women believed to be the hottest thing on legs. Stern got any woman he wanted. If anybody ought to know about a woman's appeal, it should be him.

JoJo chuckled, remembering. In high school, girls would deliberately pretend to befriend her for no other reason than to get close to Stern. It never worked for long because once Stern learned the truth he would drop them like hot potatoes. He refused to let anyone use her. To him, friendship meant more than that. If those girls didn't want to be her friend because of who she was, then he wanted no part of them.

In truth, most of the girls she'd known in high school, and even some of the women she knew now, preferred not to hang around with someone who wasn't very girly.

JoJo preferred jeans to dresses. She liked to hunt, practiced karate, could shoot a bow and arrow, and knew more about what was under the hood of a car than most guys. Of course, that last skill set had come from her father, who had been a professional mechanic. And not just any mechanic—he had been the best.

A deep lump clogged her throat. It was hard to believe he had passed away two years ago. He'd suffered a massive heart attack while doing something he loved— working on a car. Her mother had died when JoJo was eleven, so her father's death had left her parentless. She'd inherited the auto mechanic shop, which had given her the opportunity to come out of the classroom and get under the hood of a car.

After she had gotten the teaching degree her father had wanted her to get, she'd obtained a graduate degree in technical engineering. She had enjoyed being a professor at one of the local community colleges, but owning and operating the Golden Wrench was what she truly loved.

"So are we still on speaking terms?"

Stern placed a tray of tortilla chips and salsa on the table beside her. He then slid into the other rocker.

"Not sure if we are or not," she said, reaching over and grabbing a chip to dip into the salsa and then sliding the whole thing in her mouth. "I asked you a question and you didn't answer me because you assumed I wasn't serious."

Stern took a sip of beer and glanced over the can at her. "Were you serious?"

"Yes."

"Then I apologize. I honestly thought you were trying to mess with my concentration."

A smile touched her lips. "Would I do that?"

"In a heartbeat."

"Well, yes," she admitted, trying to hide her amusement. "But I didn't today. I need information."

"On how a woman could make a man want her?"

"Yes."

Stern leaned forward in his chair and pierced her with a dark, penetrating gaze. "Why?"

She lifted a brow. "Why?"

"Yes, why would you want to know something like that?"

She didn't answer right away. Instead she took a sip of her beer and looked out at the mountains. It was a beautiful September day. A red fox flashed through a cluster of pine trees before darting between a patch of woods to disappear.

After she'd gathered her thoughts, she turned back to Stern. "There's this guy who brings his car to the shop. He's sexy. Oh…is he sexy."

Stern rolled his eyes. "I'll take your word for it. Go on."

She shrugged. "That's it."

Stern frowned. "That's it?"

"Yes. I've decided I want him. The question is, how can I get him to want me, too?"

As far as Stern was concerned, the real question was, had JoJo lost her ever-loving mind? But he didn't say that. Instead, he took another sip of his beer.

He knew JoJo better than he knew anyone, and if she was determined to do something then that was it. He could help her, or she'd find help somewhere else.

"What's his name?" he asked.

She slid another chip into her mouth. "You don't need to know that. Do you tell me the name of every woman you want?"

"This is different."

"Really? In what way?"

He wasn't sure, but he just knew that it was. Using the pad of his thumb, he rubbed the tension building at his temple. "First of all, when it comes to men, you're green. And second, for you to even ask me that question means you're not ready for the kind of relationship you're going after."

She threw her head back and laughed. "Pleeze, Stern. I'll be thirty next year. Most women my age are married by now, some with children. And I don't even have a boyfriend."

He wasn't moved by that argument. "I'll be thirty-one next year and I don't have a girlfriend." When she looked over at him, he amended that statement. "Not a steady one. I like being single."

"But you do date. A lot. I'm beginning to think that most of the men in town wonder if I'm really a girl."

He studied her. There had never been any doubt in his mind that she was a girl. She had long lashes and eyes so dark they were the color of midnight. Those eyes were staring straight ahead now, looking out over the thick woods. She had her bare legs lifted in the rocker with her arms wrapped around them. Her pose emphasized the muscles in her limbs. He knew she did a lot of physical work at the shop, but the two of them also had memberships at a gym in town.

She had changed out of her hunting clothes and was wearing cut-off jeans and a short top. She had gorgeous legs, long and endless. But he knew he was one of the few men who'd ever seen them. She opened the shop at eight and closed after five. It wasn't unusual for her to work late if she had a car an owner needed. And during that whole time, she wore an auto-mechanic's uniform splattered with grease. A number of men would be surprised how she looked wearing something other than that uniform.

"You hide stuff," he finally said.

She glanced over at him, frowning. "I hide what?"

"What a nice body you have. Most of the time men see you in your work clothes."

Her frown deepened. "Well, forgive me for not wearing stilettos and a slinky dress while I change a carburetor."

A vision of that flashed through his mind and he smiled as he took a sip of beer. "Stilettos and a slinky dress? You don't have to go that far, but…"

He glanced over at her and saw she was pouting. He kind of liked it when she pouted. She looked cute.

"But what?"

"You would probably gain more men's interest if you were seen around town after hours in something other than jeans and sweats. You're a female, JoJo. Men like women who look soft and sexy once in a while."

She studied the contents of her beer bottle. "You think that might do it?"

"Probably." He suddenly sat up straight in the rocker. "I have an idea. What you need is a makeover."

"A makeover?"

"Yes, and then you need to go where your guy hangs out. In a dress that shows your legs, a new hairdo—"

"What's wrong with my hair?"

Honestly, he didn't think there was anything wrong with her hair. It was long, thick and healthy. He should know. He'd helped her wash it numerous times over the years. He loved it when she wore it down past her shoulders, but these days she rarely did.

"You have beautiful hair. You just need to show it off more. Even now you're hiding it under a cap."

He reached over and took the hat off her head. Lustrous dark brown hair tumbled to her shoulders. He smiled. "See, I like it already."

And he did. He was tempted to run his hands through it to feel the silky texture.

He leaned back and took another sip of his beer, wondering where such a tempting thought came from. This was JoJo, for heaven's sake. His best friend. He should not be thinking about how silky her hair was.

"So, you think a makeover will work?"

"Yes, but like I said, after the makeover you need to go where you think the guy's going to be—with a date. Whenever you pull it all together, I'm available."

She met his gaze. "Not sure that will work. If I'm with someone, he might not check me out."

"Most people around here know we're best friends and nothing more."

"He's new to town and probably won't know that."

Stern thought for a moment. "You're probably right. I wouldn't come on to a woman if I saw her with another man. But you want him to accept you as you are. The woman who works as a mechanic during the day and the same woman who can get all dolled up at night, right?"

"Right."

Stern smiled. "Then I suggest you let him see you with another man. Makes it obvious that you can be sexy when you want to be and that other men appreciate you. I bet once he's seen you, even if you're with me, he'll contact you for a date. And then when he does see you in your work clothes, he'll look beyond the uniform and imagine what's underneath."

Stern's smile faded. For some reason the thought of

men checking out JoJo that way, of men calling her for a date, bothered him. Suddenly, he was thinking that maybe a makeover wasn't such a great idea after all.

"That's a wonderful idea, Stern! As soon as I get back to Denver I'm going to get started on the makeover. First, I need to find out where this guy hangs out. Then I'll find the name of someone who can make me look pretty."

"You're already pretty, JoJo."

She patted his hand. "Ah, that's sweet of you to say, but you're my best friend so your opinion of my looks doesn't count. I'll get in touch with your cousin Megan for the name of her hairstylist, and it shouldn't be hard to find a makeup artist. Then, I'll go shopping. I'll get some of your other cousins and sisters-in-law to go with me because they all like to shop. I'm excited."

He took another sip of his beer. "I can tell."

Why did her interest in a man bother him? The only reason he could come up with was that she was his best friend and he didn't want to lose their special bond. He didn't want to lose *her.* What if this guy found it strange that a man and woman were best friends? What if he pushed her to end the friendship they'd shared for years?

His gut twisted. His brothers and cousins had always said they wouldn't want any girlfriend of theirs to have the sort of close relationship with another man that he and JoJo shared. What if this guy thought the same way?

Stern did not like problems, and he always preferred dealing with them head-on.

Stern frowned. "What's his name, JoJo?"

She chuckled. "You don't need his name, Stern. Besides, you'll find out soon enough when I set my plans into motion."

Stern took a sip of his beer. He couldn't wait.

* * *

Later that night, JoJo lay in bed staring up at the ceiling. Things were going better than she'd planned. When she realized back in the spring that she was developing feelings for Stern, she had been horrified. How could a woman fall in love with her best friend?

Rather suddenly, it seemed. On their last trip here to the lodge in April, she had come downstairs one morning, ready for another great day of hunting, only to find Stern still in his pajamas. Or, partly in them. He had on the bottoms but not the top. And in that instant, on that day, she'd seen him not as her best friend but as a sexy man who had the ability to stir any woman's blood. He had certainly stirred hers. She hadn't been able to stop staring at his massive shoulders, his impressively broad chest and perfect abs. And once she'd started thinking of him as a sexy man, she couldn't seem to stop. By the end of the day she'd been a basket case.

But it was more than just sexual chemistry messing with her mind. By the end of the trip she'd realized she had fallen in love with him. Maybe she'd always loved him, but until that day she had accepted their relationship as nothing more than a very close friendship. Now, her heart wanted her to admit what she'd been denying for years.

She'd known she had to come up with a plan or risk losing her best friend forever. She might have fallen in love with Stern, but she knew he didn't love her. He was one of the most eligible bachelors in Denver and his weekends were filled with dates.

So one day two months ago, when she read a romance novel a customer had left behind in the break room, an idea popped into her head. She would find another man to fall in love with, someone who could take Stern's place in her heart.

She'd been inspired by the heroine in the book, who was also in love with a man she couldn't have. To shift her focus off of the forbidden man, the heroine began dating her next-door neighbor. Eventually she fell in love with her neighbor. At the end of the book the couple married and lived happily ever after.

Okay, so it was pure fiction—but it was still an idea that had merit. On that day, JoJo had decided to become the owner of her destiny, the creator of her own happiness.

She'd just been waiting to run into someone interesting. For the next two months, she'd waited. And just when she thought she would never meet a man who could pique her interest...in drove Walter Carmichael needing a new set of spark plugs for his Porsche.

Something about him drew her attention, and he didn't have a ring on his finger. She quickly dismissed the notion that his good looks, impeccable style and suave manner reminded her of Stern.

When she did a routine customer-service follow-up call, she found that Walter had a nice phone voice, too. He had everything going for him. Now she had to make sure she had everything going for her. And the best person to help her was her best friend, the man she was trying not to love.

Two

Stern looked up when he heard a knock on his office door. "Come in."

It was Dillon, his oldest brother and CEO of Blue Ridge Land Management, a firm that had been in their family for more than forty years. Dillon was the one in charge, their brother Riley was next in command and Stern and his older brother Canyon were corporate attorneys. His cousin Adrian would be starting in a couple of months as one of the company's engineers.

Dillon entered Stern's office then closed the door behind him and leaned against it. Stern had seen that look on Dillon's face before. It usually meant he was in a world of trouble.

"Any reason for your bad mood today?" Dillon asked, staring him down. "Your first day back from vacation and I'd have thought you'd be in a good mood, not the opposite. I heard hunting went better for JoJo than for you, but please tell me that's not what has you upset. You're not a sore loser. Besides, thanks to her father, she not only knows everything there is to know about cars, she's also an expert marksman, a karate champ and a skilled archer. She's been showing you up for years."

Stern tossed a paper clip onto his desk and stared at it for a long moment before glancing up and meeting his brother's gaze. "I'm well aware of all JoJo's skills, and that's not what's bothering me. She informed me while we were on our trip that she's set her sights on another target—and it's not an elk. It's a man."

Dillon raised a brow. "Excuse me?" He moved from the door to take the chair in front of Stern's desk.

"Just what I said. So maybe I am a sore loser, Dillon. JoJo has been my best friend forever and I don't want to lose her."

Dillon stretched his long legs out in front of him. "I think you better start from the beginning."

So Stern did. Dillon said nothing while he listened attentively. When Stern was finished he said, "I think you're getting carried away and not giving JoJo credit for being the true friend that she is. I don't think there's a man alive who can come between you two or mess up your friendship. I think it says a lot that of all the people she could have gone to for advice, she came to you. She trusts your judgment."

Dillon stood. "If I were you, I wouldn't let her down. And as far as your bad mood, you know the rules, Stern. No one can bring personal garbage into the office. Canyon just got back from his honeymoon and is in a great mood, understandably so. Yet you were going at him about every idea he tossed out, just for the hell of it. You owe everyone at the meeting, especially Canyon, an apology and I expect you to give it."

Dillon then walked to the door and opened it.

"Dil?"

Dillon stopped and turned around. "Yes?"

"Thanks for keeping me in check. I'm sorry I behaved inappropriately."

Dillon nodded. "I accept your apology, Stern. Just make sure it doesn't happen again." He then walked out and closed the door behind him.

Stern rubbed his hand down his face. He could handle anybody's disappointment but Dillon's. When their parents, and uncle and aunt, died in a plane crash nearly twenty years ago, they'd left Dillon and his cousin Ramsey in charge. It hadn't been easy, especially since several Westmorelands had been younger than the age of sixteen. Together, Dillon and Ramsey worked hard and made sacrifices to keep the family together. Dillon had even gone against the State of Colorado when they tried forcing him to put the youngest four kids in foster homes. Those were just a few of the reasons why Dillon deserved his utmost admiration and respect. Even now, he helped keep the family together.

Presently, there were fifteen Denver Westmorelands. Stern's parents had had seven sons—Dillon, Micah, Jason, Riley, Canyon, Stern and Brisbane. Uncle Adam and Aunt Clarisse had had eight children: five boys— Ramsey, Zane, Derringer and the twins Aiden and Adrian—and three girls—Megan, Gemma and Bailey.

Over the past few years, everyone had gotten married except for him, the twins, Bailey and Bane. In June Megan had married Rico, a private investigator; Canyon had up and married Keisha Ashford, the mother of his two-year-old son, last month; and Riley and his fiancée, Alpha, would be getting married at the end of this month. It was still a shock to everyone that his cousin Zane, who had once sworn he would stay a bachelor for life, would marry his fiancée, Channing, over the Christmas holidays.

Stern tossed another paper clip onto the desk before picking up the phone and punching in Canyon's extension.

"This is Canyon."

"Can, I apologize for acting like a jerk in the meeting today."

There was a slight pause. Then Canyon said, "It wasn't your usual style, Stern. We haven't argued in years. What's going on with you? I leave to go on my honeymoon and come back and you're not yourself. What happened on that hunting trip with JoJo?"

Instead of answering Canyon's question, Stern said, "Let's meet for lunch and I'll call and ask Riley to join us. My treat."

"What about Dillon?"

A wry smile curved Stern's lips. "No need. He just left my office after chewing me out, so he's straight."

Canyon released a low whistle. "Glad it was you and not me."

"Hey, JoJo, we need a new set of tires for a '75 BMW and I don't think we have the model number in stock."

JoJo glanced up from her computer screen and smiled at the older man who'd stuck his head in her door. Willie Beeker had worked for the Golden Wrench for more than forty years, first with her father and now with her. He'd been set to retire the year after her father's death and she knew he'd only hung around the past couple of years to give her the help and support she needed. Although he'd trained a number of good men, any of whom could step into his shoes, no one could take his place.

She'd known Beeker all of her life. He and her father had become best friends while working together as mechanics in the army. Her father had gotten out of the military, returned home to Denver and married. Years later, the two friends hooked back up when Beeker had divorced and moved to Denver. While growing up, she'd seen Beeker as more than one of her father's outstanding employees. She'd considered him an honorary uncle.

"No problem, Beeker. I'll start checking around immediately."

Beeker entered her office. "Things were crazy off the bat this morning, and I didn't get the chance to welcome you back and ask how things went last week."

JoJo leaned back in her chair and smiled. "I brought down an elk on the third day."

"That's great, girl! You didn't make my boy too mad, did you?"

Her smile widened. "Um, maybe just a little. But Stern will be fine."

She couldn't help remembering their final days at the lodge. They'd put up their hunting rifles and pulled out the playing cards and checkerboard. He had whipped her hands down in all the games except one, and she had a feeling he'd felt sorry for her and had given her that one.

JoJo always appreciated unwinding at the lodge with Stern and this past trip had been no exception. After their first conversation about her makeover, he hadn't wanted to discuss her request again, which made her think he wasn't crazy about the idea. But he had promised his help and she couldn't ask for more than that.

"Did the 2010 Porsche come in while I was away?"

Beeker raised a brow. "No. Why?"

"Just curious. It's a nice car."

"You sure that's all you admire?"

She held Beeker's questioning gaze. "Yes." Since her father's death he'd stepped in as a surrogate father to her, but she didn't want to worry him needlessly.

Beeker nodded. "So you think he'll ever settle down and marry?"

Now it was JoJo who raised a brow. "Who?"

"Stern."

JoJo frowned. How had they moved from the driver of the Porsche to Stern? "I don't know. Why do you ask?"

Beeker shrugged. "There have been a lot of weddings in his family lately. His cousin Megan in June, Canyon last month, Riley later this month and Zane before the end of the year. The single Westmorelands seem to be falling like flies."

"Stern dates a lot, but he doesn't have an exclusive girl."

Beeker chuckled. "If anyone would know, you would." He checked his watch. "Let me know when you locate those tires so I can send Maceo to pick them up."

Maceo Armstrong was her newest employee, fresh out of mechanic school. "I will."

It took JoJo less than thirty minutes to make a few calls, find the tires and dispatch Maceo to make a run across town. It was only then that she allowed herself to consider Beeker's question about Stern. Like she'd told Beeker, Stern didn't have a serious girl right now. But she knew that didn't mean he wouldn't meet someone eventually. After all, as Beeker had said, there had been a lot of Westmoreland weddings and engagements lately. Because of her long friendship with Stern she also was close to his family.

She'd known that Canyon had been quite taken with Keisha Ashford three years ago, so his decision to marry wasn't a surprise. But she had been surprised at Megan's marriage, only because of the swiftness of the romance between her and Rico Claiborne. And Riley's and Zane's decisions to marry were definitely shockers. Could such a thing happen to Stern? What if Stern began seeing a woman seriously and the woman convinced him to end his close friendship with JoJo out of jealousy? So far it hadn't happened, probably because none of the women he dated saw her as a threat.

Stern would be a good catch for any woman. Besides being handsome and wealthy, he was a nice person—insightful, kind and considerate. And she didn't just think that because he was her best friend. He dated a lot, but he never treated any woman shabbily. He let them know up front where he stood in regards to relationships and he'd said more than once that he had no intention of settling down or thinking about marriage until after his thirty-fifth birthday. That meant he only had five years to go. And he'd only have that much time if some woman didn't come along to sweep him off his feet. JoJo had never worried about that before, but the family trend seemed to be that the Westmoreland men were vulnerable to love.

JoJo shook her head. *Vulnerable?* She couldn't imagine that word connected to Riley or Zane. And because she knew them so well, she figured that if they were making a long-term commitment, it was because they deeply loved the woman they were marrying.

And because Stern never did anything half-step, there was no doubt in her mind that one day he would meet a woman and fall in love just as deeply. And when that happened, where would it leave her? She knew the answer without having to think hard about it.

Alone.

That meant she had to move forward with her plan. It would be imperative to have someone special of her own before Stern met someone and married. Pushing away from the desk, she stretched her body before grabbing a clipboard off the wall. As she left her office she knew pursuing Walter Carmichael was more important than ever. In a few days she would know where he liked to hang out and then go from there. Wanda, her fiftysomething-year-old know-it-all receptionist, was on it and if anyone could find out the information it would be her.

Like Beeker, Wanda was another trusted employee who'd worked for the Golden Wrench for years—ever since JoJo was in high school. It had been Wanda who had explained to JoJo why it meant so much to her father that she take those etiquette classes and dance lessons, although she'd hated every minute of them. She much preferred being under the hood of a car instead of acting like a simpering idiot the way most teen girls behaved. She and her father had compromised. He would let her go hunting with him and Beeker and take the karate and archery classes she loved, if she learned what she needed to know to be a lady every once in a while.

She'd never been interested in boys the way other girls had been, mainly because the boys sought her out and not the other way around—it hadn't been for her looks, but for her wheels. Thanks to her dad, she'd always driven a smooth-looking muscle car, a guy's dream. And just as Stern had known the girls' motives for faking friendship with her, she'd been very much aware of the guys' motives. That was yet another reason her friendship with Stern meant so much to her.

Whether it happened in a few months or in the next year, one day he would be forced to end their friendship. And the last thing she wanted him to do was feel guilty about having to cut her loose.

Then there was that other problem she'd found herself contending with during their weekend away: her new-found attraction to him. More than once while they'd been playing cards, when his attention was squarely on the hand he held, her attention had been squarely on him. When had that little mole on his upper lip started to look so sexy? And when had long eyelashes on a man become a turn-on?

If those thoughts weren't bad enough, when he had dropped her off at home and given her the usual peck on the cheek and hug, she had felt her heart pounding deep in her chest. Yes, she was into Stern bad, and the only way out of it was to turn her attention to another man.

Still, the memory of Stern singing in the shower, whistling through the lodge while he cooked breakfast or humming late at night while they sat together on the deck playing checkers was embedded in her brain.

She was so lost in remembering that she didn't slow her pace when she rounded the corner until her body hit the solid wall of a man's chest.

"Whoa. Going to a fire, Jo?" Stern asked, reaching out to steady her.

She seemed to blush, and he couldn't help wondering what she had been thinking about. He had a feeling her thoughts hadn't been on work.

"Stern, what are you doing here?" she asked, sounding somewhat breathless.

He lifted a brow. "Any reason I shouldn't be here?" he asked, releasing her and then turning to fall in step beside her.

"No, but it's Monday and we just got back yesterday."

"I know but I met Riley and Canyon for lunch at Mc-Kays, and thought I'd check to see how things are going since I was in the neighborhood."

"Oh."

Was that disappointment he heard in her voice? Did she wish it had been that other guy—the one whose name she refused to give him—to show up unexpectedly and not him? That thought didn't sit well with him. "You don't sound too happy to see me."

She glanced over at him. "Don't be silly. I'm always happy to see you."

He didn't say anything for a moment. Was he being silly? Was the whole issue silly—the very issue that had nagged at him and kept him up last night to the point where he had snapped at his brothers this morning? Had he gotten chewed out by his oldest brother for nothing?

Pushing those questions to the back of his mind, he asked her, "What are your plans for later?"

"Um, nothing. I haven't unpacked yet and will probably do that and laundry. Why?"

"No reason."

They entered one of the bays where Beeker and another one of her employees had a car up on the lift changing out the struts. Stern greeted the men as he and JoJo passed through.

"How many cars do you have to work on today?" he asked as he continued following her to the bay she normally used. He watched as she glanced down at her clipboard. "So far there are only five scheduled. But you know how that might end up on a Monday."

Yes, he knew. Back in high school, when her father was alive, he and JoJo had been hired out to do odds and ends in the shop. He had enjoyed learning from her father and Beeker and all the other guys. And Wanda had been a hoot. JoJo's father's death had hit him as much as it had hit her. Joseph Jones had been a man Stern had looked up to, a man he had respected, a man who'd spent a lot of time with him.

Stern had spent as many days and nights with JoJo and her father as he had at home. He'd gone on hunting trips with them. Mr. Jones had taught him the proper way to handle a gun and Beeker had taught him and JoJo how to shoot.

"You want to take in a movie tomorrow night?"

She glanced up at him and he wondered why, in all the years he'd known her, he had just realized how mesmerizing her eyes were.

"A movie?"

"Yes." They'd gone to movies together a number of times, too many to count, and never had they considered them dates or anything more than two friends hanging out. Why did he suddenly feel that this invitation was different?

"What's playing?" she asked, eyeing him suspiciously. "The past couple of times we went to a movie we saw ones that none of your girlfriends wanted to see. So you took me. Must be one of those blood and guts flicks."

He couldn't help but chuckle because she knew him so well. "There is this new action movie that came out this weekend. Riley claims it's good."

"And the reason you can't find a date for tomorrow?"

"Not trying to find one. We still need to talk."

"About what?" she asked, checking her watch.

"About that request you asked of me at the lodge."

She stopped walking and hung the clipboard at its designated place on the wall. "If I remember correctly, you didn't want to talk about it."

She was right. The more he thought about the makeover, the more he thought it wasn't a good idea. If a man only cared about outside appearances, then he might not get to know the JoJo that Stern knew from the inside out. She had a heart of gold, and she was cheating herself if she pursued a man who would only zero in on her looks.

But he knew JoJo and she had made up her mind

about this guy whose name she refused to give him. The thought of this unnamed man made him mad, and then madder each and every time he thought about him. So Stern decided that the best thing to do was to keep an eye on her and make sure she didn't get into trouble or into any situation she couldn't handle.

"Well, I do want to talk about it now, and I'm thinking a makeover might not work after all."

She frowned. "Why?"

He shoved his hands in his pockets. "Your mystery man won't get to know the real you."

She rolled her eyes. "He can get to know the real me later. First, I need to get him to notice me. So I think the makeover will work, and you did say you would help me. Don't try wiggling out of it now."

"I'm not." He paused. "I just don't want you to get hurt."

"Hurt?" She glanced around as if to make sure none of her employees were within hearing range. "Are you saying you don't think that a makeover will help me? That I'm so much of a reject that even a makeover wouldn't do me any good?"

"No, that's not what—"

"Well I've got news for you, Stern. I've seen even the ugliest of women and men become beautiful and handsome. So there's no reason to believe a makeover can't do wonders for me, too."

"That's not what I was insinuating, JoJo."

"Doesn't matter. I'll show you," she said, then walked off toward the first car she would be working on.

He rubbed his hand down his face in frustration. What was going on here? He and JoJo never fought or argued about anything, and now they seemed to be bickering back and forth about every damn thing.

All he'd said was that he didn't want to see her hurt. Why would she think he'd meant that a makeover wouldn't help her? In truth, he knew it would help her and that's what he was worried about. Men would be coming on to her for all the wrong reasons.

He glanced over at her as she leaned over the car to look under the hood. He couldn't help noticing how her work pants stretched tightly over her backside. Her perfectly shaped backside. Damn, why was he checking out JoJo?

He drew in a frustrated breath. "I'll call you later."

"Whatever," she mumbled without even bothering to look up.

Stern left, feeling as if he'd made the situation between them worse instead of better.

Three

"Here's the information you wanted on that Carmichael dude."

JoJo looked up into the face of a petite blonde who didn't look her age. A copy of Wanda's birth certificate in her employment file indicated she was nearing sixty, but if you asked Wanda she would swear she wasn't even fifty yet. And since she had the face and figure to back it up, no one had dared to call her on it.

JoJo picked up the card Wanda had tossed on her desk. "He lives in Cherry Hills Village." The Village was one of the most affluent suburbs in Denver.

"You're surprised? Look how he dresses. Look at the car he drives. Not to mention what he does for a living."

JoJo nodded. "He's thirty-one, the same age as Stern. And according to what you've found out, he's not in an exclusive relationship."

"Also like Stern."

JoJo shifted her gaze from the card to Wanda, who was pretending to peruse JoJo's bulletin board. She'd known Wanda long enough to recognize the smile the older woman was trying to hide. "Well, yes," JoJo admitted. "Like Stern."

Wanda tilted her head and met JoJo's gaze. "Come to think of it, there's a lot about this Carmichael man that would remind a person of Stern. Is there a reason for that?"

JoJo decided she didn't want to hold Wanda's gaze any longer. The woman was sharp. "What do you think?"

JoJo couldn't resist watching Wanda out of the corners of her eyes. She saw Wanda look thoughtful for a moment before she said, "Do you really want me to tell you what I think, Jovonnie?"

JoJo tried to ignore the tension building at her temples. Whenever Wanda called her by her full name JoJo knew Wanda would go into "it's time I tell it the way I see it" mode.

"Don't you have a switchboard to cover? You are on payroll," she reminded her.

"Don't try pulling rank on me, young lady. This is my lunch break, and need I remind you I am entitled to one?"

"No you don't have to remind me, but I'm working through mine, so if you don't mind, I—"

"I do mind," Wanda interrupted, resting her hip on the edge of JoJo's desk. "And the reason I mind is because I think you're making a big mistake."

Seeing that she wouldn't be getting any work done until Wanda had her say, JoJo tossed her pen on her desk and leaned back in her chair. "Evidently, you want to get something off your chest."

"I do."

JoJo nodded. "All right, you have the floor." She placed the card down on her desk.

Taking JoJo at her word, Wanda stood and paced in front of JoJo's desk. Wanda was a beautiful woman who had gone through two marriages. The first had ended in death and the other in divorce. Wanda would tell anyone that the second marriage had been a mistake because she'd tried to find a man who could replace a husband who was irreplaceable.

Wanda had fallen in love with a cop at the age of twenty-one, and he'd left her a widow with a newborn baby at twenty-eight. She had remarried at thirty-four and divorced at thirty-seven. She and her ex were both still single and remained friends. It wasn't unusual for him to drop by the shop every so often to take Wanda to lunch or dinner.

Tension now throbbed at JoJo's temples. She had a ton of paperwork to do, and like she'd told Stern, she needed to go home to unpack and do laundry. She'd become impatient with the pacing when Wanda finally stopped, snagged her gaze and said, "You've fallen in love with Stern."

JoJo was glad her backside was firmly planted in the chair or she would have fallen out of it. She was totally positive she hadn't given her feelings away so how had Wanda figured things out? JoJo didn't want to believe what her father had always jokingly said about Wanda: that she had a sixth sense about stuff that wasn't any of her business.

When JoJo didn't say anything, but just sat there and stared, Wanda said, "Admit it."

JoJo quickly snapped out of her moment of stunned silence. She reached across her desk and picked up the pen she'd tossed aside earlier and pretended to jot something down on one of the documents she picked up. "I won't admit anything. Don't be silly."

"Not silly, just observant. And you should know by now that I don't miss a thing."

JoJo replaced her pen on the desk and tilted her head. "And just what do you think you haven't been missing?"

Wanda smiled. "The way you've started looking at Stern when you think he won't notice. The way you smile whenever you see him. How excited you were to go on that hunting trip with him. You acted like it was your first time when you do it two or three times a year."

JoJo waved off her words. "All circumstantial evidence."

"Yes, but then you decide to check out a guy who could be Stern's clone. To me that's an obvious sign."

JoJo nibbled on her bottom lip before allowing a frown to settle on her face. "You make me sound pathetic."

Wanda shook her head. "Not pathetic. Just confused."

Now it was JoJo who needed to stand. Instead of pacing, she moved to the window. It was a beautiful September day, but all she had to do was look up at the high mountains to know Denver would get an early winter. And a pretty cold one, too.

She turned around and, not surprisingly, she found Wanda leaning her hips on JoJo's desk. "Let's just say your theory is true. Mind you, I'm not saying that it is," JoJo said. "But let's say, for the sake of argument, that it is. What's wrong with me moving toward a sure thing instead of getting hung up on a lost cause?"

"Why would you think Stern is a lost cause?"

JoJo thought long and hard about Wanda's question before answering. "He's only a lost cause when it pertains to me. I know him. He's my best friend, and he knows that's all he'll ever be to me. There's no need for me to waste my time wanting more. Knowing that, I'd go to a plan that might work."

"Walter Carmichael?"

"Yes. He's just what I need to move ahead in another direction." *Away from Stern.*

"And what if that doesn't work?"

JoJo smiled. "It will. I intend to learn from the best."

Wanda stared at her for a minute. "Please tell me you're not doing what I think you're doing."

JoJo shrugged as she went back to her desk and sat down. "Okay, I won't tell you."

Wanda shook her head. "It's not going to work, JoJo. When one man has your heart you can't replace him with another. I learned that the hard way."

JoJo watched as Wanda squared her shoulders and walked out of the office. One day, JoJo decided, she would have a long talk with Wanda and get the facts about what had happened with her second marriage. Why had it been so difficult to move on and fall in love again with a good man?

JoJo was certain it wouldn't be that hard for her to shift her affections from Stern to Walter. She'd never been married to Stern, after all. Falling for another man shouldn't be difficult.

In a way, she was looking forward to showing up at the Punch Bowl on Saturday night. From the information Wanda had just provided her with, it seemed that's where Walter hung out on the weekends. She'd heard it had live entertainment and was a nice place to dance, a place where women went to meet men.

She drew in a deep breath knowing this weekend she would be in that number.

"This must be serious." Zane Westmoreland opened the door to his cousin.

Stern walked past him and into the living room. "What makes you think that?"

Zane shrugged as he followed. "You're here. I can't recall the last time you came visiting."

"You've had a house guest and I didn't want to intrude. I heard she's gone for now." Stern was talking about the woman Zane would be marrying over the holidays. Stern was still somewhat in shock about that. If anyone had told him that his cousin Zane, the one man who not only knew women like the back of his hand but who also enjoyed them tremendously, would settle down and marry, Stern would not have believed them.

"Channing had to go back to Atlanta for work. She'll be moving here from Atlanta permanently next month."

"Think you can last until then?"

Zane smiled. "Not sure. She'll be back in a few weeks for Riley's wedding. We'll spend Thanksgiving with her folks and then we marry on Christmas Day."

"Sounds like you have it all planned out," Stern said, sitting on the couch and stretching his long legs in front of him.

"I do." There was a pause. "So what brings you by on a Monday night, Stern?"

Stern would think the reason he'd stopped by was obvious. Zane, who was six years older, had a reputation for knowing women. Not just a little about them but practically everything. Before he'd become engaged to Channing, Zane had been the family expert on the subject, and Stern figured the kind of knowledge Zane possessed didn't dissipate with an engagement.

"It's JoJo."

Zane's brow lifted. "What about JoJo?"

Stern released a slow breath. JoJo had been his best friend for years so everyone in the family knew her. "She asked me for a favor."

"What kind of favor?"

"She wanted me to tell her how to make a man want her. There's this guy she's been checking out. Only thing is, he doesn't seem to reciprocate the interest, so she wants me to tell her what she needs to do to stimulate that interest."

Zane nodded. "Oh, I see."

Stern frowned. "Well, I sure as hell don't."

"You wouldn't."

Stern's frown deepened. "What is that supposed to mean?"

A slight smile touched Zane's lips. "It means that since JoJo's your best friend, you're too close to the situation. If you were another woman it wouldn't be a big deal, but because you're a man, to you it is a big deal."

"Of course it's a big deal. Why should she worry about making a man want her? If the guy doesn't have the sense to want her on his own, why should she worry about it?"

"Because she evidently wants him and wants him to want her in return. There's nothing wrong with that."

Stern figured there was a lot wrong with it.

"So what did you tell her?" Zane asked.

Stern leaned back against the sofa cushions. "When I didn't take her seriously at first, she copped an attitude. That's the last thing I needed so I offered a few pointers. I told her that she probably should wear more dresses. JoJo has great legs, and she should flaunt them more. I also suggested she stop hiding her hair under a cap. Her hair is one of her strong points. I particularly like it when she wears it down."

Zane nodded again. "Anything else?"

"I told her that after her makeover, she should find out where this guy hangs out and go there, impress him as the new and improved JoJo. I told her if she decided to make such a move then I would go with her."

"Why?"

Stern's brow bunched in confusion. "Why?"

"Yes, why? Why do you feel the need to go with her?"

"Because I don't know the guy," he said defensively. "She won't give me his name or tell me anything about him, other than that he brings his car in to get it serviced from time to time."

"That's all you need to know. If you ask me, that's more than you should know. JoJo is a grown woman who can take care of herself."

"You don't know that."

Zane chuckled. "We're talking about JoJo, Stern. The same woman who can hit a target with a gun *or* a bow and arrow with one eye closed. The same woman who has a black belt. You and I both know she can take care of herself, so that means there's something else bothering you. What is it?"

Stern frowned as he stared at the floor and mumbled, "Nothing."

Zane didn't say anything for a minute. "There is something, Stern. You didn't come here because you wanted to see my pug face. There's something bothering you, so come clean. I can only help if you do that."

Stern paused. "I'm afraid, Zane."

Zane lifted a brow. "Afraid? What are you afraid of?"

"That I'm going to lose my best friend. What if she gets serious with this guy and he has a problem with our relationship? You've said enough times that you wouldn't want any woman of yours to share the kind of relationship with a man that JoJo shares with me."

"You won't lose her," Zane said, trying to reassure him.

"You can't be certain of that, and I can't take that chance."

Zane shook his head. "You're going to have to trust her judgment."

"I trust hers. I just don't trust his."

Zane rolled his eyes. "But you don't know him."

"Exactly," Stern said, standing. "That's why I need to find out who he is and check him out."

"I think you're going at it all wrong."

"I don't," he said, heading for the door. "Bye, Zane. You've given me a lot to think about."

"No, I didn't. I suggest you examine your own feelings for JoJo," Zane replied. But Stern was already out the door and didn't hear what his cousin had said.

The next night JoJo stepped onto her porch and inhaled deeply to fill her lungs with crisp mountain air. She had put her hair in a ponytail before placing her favorite Denver Broncos cap on her head, but instead of her usual jeans and T-shirt, she was wearing a blue blouse and a pair of black corduroy slacks. She'd also grabbed a jacket because the evenings were turning cool.

She heard a sound, turned and then smiled at the man coming up the steps. Her heart raced. Stern's well-toned physique was displayed in a pair of jeans, a blue Western shirt and a Stetson. He looked way too handsome for his own good.

She checked her watch. "You're on time."

"Aren't I always?" Stern said, glancing around. "I hope you don't stand out here on the porch waiting for all your dates."

JoJo adjusted her cap. "You aren't a date. Come on," she said, grabbing his arm and heading down the steps. "I've already locked up and turned on the alarm. The movie starts in twenty minutes."

"Whoa, what's the rush? There's not much traffic out so we'll make it."

She knew he was right, but she was looking forward to tonight. Any time she got to spend with Stern made her all giggly inside. She was certain those feelings would pass once she knew more about Walter. And speaking of Walter...

"I'm going to get that makeover this weekend," she said as she got into the car and buckled her seat belt.

Stern glanced over at her after buckling his own. "Why?"

She felt the huge smile that spread across her face. "I found out where my guy hangs out on the weekend and I plan to show up."

Stern held her gaze for a moment and then asked, "Where?"

"I'll tell you only if you promise not to show up."

"Not making that promise, JoJo."

She rolled her eyes. "Then I won't tell you. Why are you being difficult about this, Stern? Do I show up at places where I know you'll be taking your dates?"

"No. But I'm not the one asking for advice on how to reel someone in. Besides, I want to make sure he doesn't get disrespectful with you," Stern said, pulling out of her driveway.

She frowned. "Dammit, Stern, I can take care of myself. If I can catch his attention, we'll talk, listen to music and dance. It shouldn't be hard to tell if he's interested."

He turned to her when the car came to a traffic light. "But he'll be interested for the wrong reason."

"I can handle it."

He grunted. "So you're really going to go through with this?"

"Yes. Of course. I thought we cleared up the issue of

how serious I was last week." He was acting too much like a big brother to suit her.

A couple of hours later, to her way of thinking, Stern was not in the best of moods. The movie was good and she had enjoyed it, but each time she stole a glance at him, he was frowning.

"That sour look will get stuck in place if you don't get rid of it, Stern," she teased as they walked out of the theater.

He looked over at her. "Funny."

"You don't see me laughing. The movie was your idea, but I don't think you enjoyed being here," she said, sliding into the car when he opened the door for her.

"I enjoyed the movie, and I enjoyed your company."

JoJo wasn't convinced. She glanced at her watch. "It's early. You want to drop by McKays for coffee?"

"That sounds good."

At least he wasn't in a rush to get her home, she thought. "I talked to Megan about the guy that does her hair, and she suggested I talk to Pam, so I'm doing that tomorrow. I hope she'll be able to recommend someone who can do my makeover. She always looks good. In fact, all the women your cousins and brothers married look great."

Pam was married to his oldest brother, Dillon. A former movie star who'd been a regular on one of JoJo's favorite soaps years ago, Pam had given it all up to return to her home in Wyoming to raise her three younger sisters when her father died. That was when she'd met Dillon.

"What if I told you I like the way you look?" Stern said, intruding on her thoughts.

She rolled her eyes. "You would since you're my best friend. Besides, I'm not trying to impress you, remember? However, I appreciate the fact that you gave me some advice at the lodge. It's advice that I'm putting to good use since I consider you an expert on what men like. I'm going shopping on Friday, and after talking to Pam I'll be contacting someone who can perform miracles on my hair and help with my makeup."

He didn't say anything. He just redirected his focus on the road. But she would swear she could hear his teeth gnashing. Why was he upset about her setting her sights on a guy? When minutes passed and she could feel the tension radiating between them, she couldn't stand it any longer. When he pulled into McKays' parking lot and brought the car to a stop, she turned to him as she unbuckled her seat belt. "What's wrong with you, Stern? I thought you understood. Why do you have a problem with me going after a guy I want when you do the same with any woman you want?"

Stern didn't say anything for a long moment. "Is it wrong for me to want to protect you, JoJo?"

She drew in a deep breath. Little did he know, she was trying to protect him…mainly from herself. If Stern had any idea that she'd fallen in love with him, he would probably race toward the nearest mountain, away from her.

"It's wrong if I don't want to be protected. You're acting worse than Dad ever did. Even he had the good sense to loosen the binds when I got older. In fact, he would tell me all the time that I needed to get out more, date, get dressed up and meet boys. He didn't worry about me because he knew I could take care of myself. Why don't you?"

"That's not it."

She lifted a brow. "Then what is it?"

Stern frowned, not knowing if he could explain how he felt without sounding selfish. Was he willing to deny her a chance to be happy just because he didn't want to lose her? "Nothing. I'm just in a bad mood. Sorry."

He started to open the car door to get out when she reached out and touched his arm. "Why are you in a bad mood?"

He shrugged. "Craziness at the office. My first day back yesterday didn't go well." No need to tell her how he'd been a jerk in front of his brothers and how Dillon had read him the riot act. "Work was piled high on my desk. I have a lot of cases to prepare for this week. A ton of stuff to do with little time."

He saw the sympathetic look in her eyes and felt like a heel for stretching the truth. The number of files on his desk was manageable and had nothing to do with his mood.

She patted his hand. "Don't worry about it, Stern. You can do it. You always do. You're bright. Intelligent. A hard worker. And you have a good head on your shoulders."

He couldn't respond. What she'd said was the JoJo way. She'd always had the ability to make him believe in himself even when the odds were stacked against him. Like when he'd wanted to play basketball in high school but his grades hadn't been the best. She had tutored him and when he'd wanted to give up, she wouldn't let him. She'd encouraged him by saying some of the same things to him then that she had said just now. And, dammit, she always had him believing it. "Thanks, JoJo."

How in the world had he been blessed with a best friend like her? A lot of people considered them odd because of their unique friendship. And there were some, like his cousins Bailey and the twins—Aiden and Adrian—who thought they would eventually become more than friends. He had told them time and time again that he didn't see JoJo that way. She was his best friend and nothing more. He refused to think anything had changed.

"Ready to go inside?" he asked her.

"Yes, I can use the coffee. I need to finish inventory. We're running out of supplies too soon. Something isn't adding up."

"Then I'm sure you'll find out what the problem is," he said, getting out of the car. "You're always on top of stuff."

He came around the car to open the door for her. "Thanks for the vote of confidence," she said.

"No problem."

Pushing the car door shut behind her, he took her hand and together they moved toward the entrance of Mc-Kays, a popular restaurant in town. It was only when they were inside and greeted by the hostess that he released JoJo's hand.

And only then did it occur to him how good it had felt holding it.

"Thanks for the movie and coffee tonight, Stern."

"Don't mention it," he said, following her inside her home. Whenever he took her out, he would come in with her and check things out.

After their little discussion in which he had explained why he was in such a bad mood, his attitude had vastly improved. Over coffee, he'd joked about Aiden and Adrian and their plans now that they had finished college. Aiden, who had gone into the medical field, was doing his residency at a hospital in Maine. Adrian, who'd gotten a master's degree in engineering, would start working for Blue Ridge as a project engineer in a couple of months.

Adrian had decided to travel abroad before returning to Denver to settle down and start work.

She and Stern also talked about all the excitement swirling around the Westmoreland households, with all the recent marriages and engagements. The one thing she noted was that Stern thought it was really funny that some of his cousins and brothers figured he would be next—even though he didn't have a steady girlfriend.

"Everything checks out," Stern said, coming out of her kitchen.

"Only because you scared away the bogeyman." She chuckled and took off her cap, tossing it on a table before removing the band from her hair to let the waves flow around her shoulders. She wondered if the person who would do her hair for the weekend would suggest cutting it. She'd never gotten her hair cut, but if it meant getting Walter to notice her, then she would definitely consider it.

JoJo almost jumped at the feel of Stern's hand in her hair. She hadn't heard him cross the room.

"I love your hair," he said softly, running his fingers through the strands.

His fingers felt good. "I know," she said. He had always complimented her on her hair and she knew from their conversation at the lodge that he thought she shouldn't hide it under a cap.

"Tell me you won't cut it. Ever."

"Umm, can't do that. The hairstylist might suggest I cut it as part of the makeover."

When she heard his teeth gnashing she glanced up at him. They were standing closer than she'd realized. "You're supporting me with all this, right?" she asked, trying to sound in control of herself, of her emotions. Why did he have to smell so good?

He didn't say anything as he continued to run his fingers through her hair. Why was heat beginning to flow through her? It's not like he'd never played with her hair before. When they were younger he would pull her pigtails all the time, and then when she got older, her pigtails became ponytails and he would pull those, too. And more than a few times he'd helped her wash her hair when they'd vacationed at the lodge. But that was before she'd discovered she had feelings for him, before she'd begun lusting after him. Some of her dreams about him were totally X-rated.

She cleared her throat. "Well, if you still plan to go into the office early, you better go home and get a good night's sleep. And I still have those inventory reports to go over before I can call it a night."

"Yes, you're right," he said, pulling his fingers from her hair and checking his watch. "It's getting late."

"Yes, it is." Was it her imagination or did his voice sound a little throatier than usual? He was still standing there, and he had reached back up to run his fingers through her hair again. Why was her body shifting closer to him? Why was her face tilting toward his?

More heat streaked up her spine and she was swathed in feelings she had never felt before.

And then Stern's fingers tightened on several strands of her hair and he lowered his mouth to hers.

She leaned up to meet his lips, feeling weak in the knees as their lips touched. Sensing she was about to lose her balance, Stern wrapped his arms around her and deepened the kiss. At least she had the presence of mind to grip his shoulders. Voices echoed through her brain: *this is wrong. This is Stern. He's my best friend and we shouldn't be engaging in this sort of thing.* But she ignored the voices as sensations overtook her.

And then he did something that made her gasp in

shock. He deepened the kiss even more, literally sucking her tongue into his mouth and devouring it. Never had she been kissed this way. To be honest, she'd never really been kissed at all. That sloppy, wet kiss Mitch Smith had planted on her lips right before Stern had clobbered him, when they'd been in the tenth grade, was nothing compared to this. In fact, it was crap compared to this.

This was the kind of kiss that romance novel authors wrote about—the kind that rendered you senseless and boneless at the same time. She couldn't help wondering if this was a test. Stern knew about her inexperience when it came to men, yet she had boldly set her sights on a man. Was he kissing her merely to show her what to expect? To see how good—or awful—she was?

That wasn't a bad idea, she thought. Then he could give her pointers so she wouldn't mess things up with Walter. Yes, that had to be it. That had to be the reason he was kissing her like this. He was kissing her to give her suggestions afterward. In that case…

She tightened her hands on his shoulders and leaned into him as he sucked on her tongue. She hadn't known a kiss could be so intense until now, and she liked it. It made her pulse throb and heat circle continuously in her belly.

To say she'd lived a sheltered life would be an understatement, but it had been her own choosing. Instead of going away to school, she had remained in Denver to attend college and had even stayed at home, preferring that to living on campus. Her father had tried talking her into going away to school, saying she needed to see the world. But she had convinced him that she was perfectly fine living with him.

She'd never experimented with men. Having her first

experiment be with Stern made more streaks of heat rush up her spine as his tongue continued to tangle with hers.

Why were her hips instinctively moving against his? Why was such a reaction causing shivers to overtake her?

The need to take a deep breath caused her to pull her mouth away.

"Wow," she heard him say and watched him lick his lips.

Drawing in much-needed air, she met his gaze. "Well, how did I do?"

He raised a brow. "Excuse me?"

"How did I do? You were testing me, right?"

He shook his head as if to clear it. "Testing you?"

"Yes. You of all people know how green I am when it comes to kissing. I figured you didn't want me to embarrass myself when I let Walter kiss me. So how did I do?"

"Walter?"

Too late, JoJo realized she'd let the man's name slip. But all Stern had was a first name and there were plenty of Walters out there. "Just tell me how I did."

He stared at her for a long moment and then said, "A little more practice wouldn't hurt."

"Oh," she said, feeling disappointed.

"But you surprised me. You're better than I thought."

Her face then split into a wide smile. "I am?"

"Yes."

She nodded, moving from feeling disappointed to feeling elated. "Thanks. I was worried there for a minute."

"Don't be. With a little more practice you'd be off the charts. Now about this Walter…"

If he thought she would tell him anything else he had another think coming. "Don't ask me anything about him, Stern," she said. "Let's get back to talking about the kiss."

He crossed his arms over his chest. "What about it? I said you're good."

"You also said with practice I'd be better. And I want to be better. That means I'll need you to teach me how to be a better kisser."

"For this Walter?"

There was no need to lie about it so she said, "Yes, for Walter."

"In other words," he said as if he needed to make sure they were on the same page, "you want to learn to kiss to impress this Walter guy."

She nodded. Isn't that what she'd said? "Yes."

He just stood there and stared at her for a full minute and she had to force herself not to tremble under his laser-sharp gaze. When he didn't say anything and only continued to look at her, she began nibbling on her bottom lip.

"Well? Will you help me improve?"

"I'll think about it. Now come on and let me out. I'm leaving."

JoJo followed him to the door. "When will you let me know, Stern? I don't have much time."

When he reached the door he turned to her. "Soon." He leaned in to place the customary peck on her cheek. "Don't stay up too late."

Then he opened the door and she watched him leave.

Four

"Any reason you're banging on my door at this hour? It's after midnight, Stern," Zane said, moving aside to let his cousin enter.

Stern went straight into the living room and began pacing. Zane stared at him before plopping down on the sofa. He rubbed his hand down his face. "You want a cup of coffee?"

Stern stopped pacing and stared at him. "No, what I want is advice. I had a date with JoJo tonight."

Zane leaned back against the sofa cushion. "You have dates with JoJo all the time. What made tonight different?"

"I kissed her."

Zane stared at him for a moment, shook his head and then said, "I think we better drink coffee after all. If you don't need a cup, I do." He stood and walked toward the kitchen with Stern following in his wake. Once he set the coffeemaker on and it began brewing, he turned to Stern and leaned against the counter. "So, now do you want to tell me why you kissed JoJo?"

Stern shoved his hands into his pockets. "I don't know why I kissed her. I was playing with her hair one minute and then the next thing I knew, I was practically shoving my tongue down her throat."

"No graphics, please," Zane said, pouring a cup of coffee and then moving toward the table to sit down.

"Well, that's what happened."

"I'm surprised JoJo didn't karate chop you."

Stern decided he needed a cup of coffee after all and went over to the counter to pour a cup. "She didn't because she thought I was testing her."

"Testing her?"

"Yes. She's doing a makeover for that guy I was telling you about. His name is Walter, by the way. She let it slip out. But I don't know his last name."

Zane shook his head. "You're digressing. Please go back to why JoJo thinks she was being tested?"

Stern joined Zane at the table. "Because I know she's never really been kissed, she figured I was testing her to make sure she knew what to do when this Walter guy kisses her. Then, I made the mistake of telling her that she needs to improve on her kisses."

"Does she?"

"Hell, no, I lied. She was good. Too damn good. To be honest with you, the kiss was off the charts. And now the lie has caught up with me because she wants me to help her become a better kisser."

Zane stared at him for a long moment. "Let me get this straight. You and JoJo have a platonic relationship to the degree that she thinks the two of you can practice kissing without anything happening?"

"Nothing will happen," Stern argued.

Zane snorted. "If you believed that you wouldn't be

here, sitting at my table after midnight on a weeknight needing advice."

Stern knew that to be true. "To answer your question, yes she thinks our relationship is platonic to that degree because she sees me as nothing more than a friend. Her best friend."

"Well, can you handle teaching her to improve her kissing?"

Stern stared down into his cup of coffee and then he said, "That's the weird thing, Zane. Tonight, when I was kissing JoJo, one part of my brain kept saying...*Hey, this is JoJo you're locking lips with.* But then another part was tasting a very sensuous woman. A woman who has her sights on another man. While I was kissing her I forgot she was my best friend."

"Sounds like you've gotten yourself in a mess."

"Don't I know it? If I refuse to do it, she's going to think I'm being selfish and don't want her with Walter because I'm being overprotective. But if I do what she's asking, I might lose control and want to take it to another level. A level that can't exist between best friends. So what do you suggest?"

Zane rubbed his chin in deep thought. Then he said, "Do what she wants."

Stern frowned. "You want me to teach her how to kiss for some other man? That Walter guy?"

Zane took a sip of his coffee. "No. If you were smart, you would teach her how to kiss for yourself."

"This isn't funny, Zane."

"And you don't see me laughing, Stern."

Stern stared long and hard at him. "Are you suggesting that after all these years I consider moving from best friends to lovers with JoJo?"

Zane smiled. "Yes, I guess I am."

Anger raced through Stern. "You're off your rocker to suggest such a thing. There's no way I can do that. That's pure crazy."

Zane chuckled. "You kissed her tonight, and I gather you rather enjoyed it. I'm sure this time yesterday the thought of doing such a thing would have been pure crazy."

Stern frowned as he stood up. "I'm leaving. I came here for advice—not for you to get ridiculous on me."

"And you think I'm being ridiculous?" Zane asked.

"Yes. How long have JoJo and I been best friends, Zane?"

"A long time. Since middle school, if I recall."

"You're recalling right. And in all those years, at any time, did you suspect there was ever more between us?" Stern asked, certain what Zane's response would be.

"Sure. All of us have."

Stern frowned. That wasn't the response he'd expected. "And who exactly is *all of us?*"

Zane shrugged massive shoulders. "Mostly everybody."

Stern stared at Zane for several long seconds while Zane sipped his coffee as if it didn't bother him that he was being stared at. "Well, I hope *mostly everybody* knows they are wrong. JoJo and I have never been anything but the best of friends. I will protect her with my life and vice versa. I have never, ever thought of her as anything other than my best friend."

"So what was the kiss about tonight? You said she thought she was being tested, but I'm curious to know what you thought you were doing. Locking lips with a woman who is nothing more than your best friend? Shoving your tongue down her throat...and those were your words, not mine."

Tension began to build at Stern's temples. He pushed his cup of coffee aside and stood up. "I'm leaving."

"You didn't answer my question," Zane pointed out. "What was the kiss about tonight? Why did you kiss her in the first place?"

"I told you what happened. I was playing with her hair one minute and then the next thing I knew, I was kissing her."

"Playing with her hair? Interesting. Do you do that often?"

"Yes. No. Stop it, Zane! You're confusing me."

"And you're confusing me, Stern. It's after midnight and I'm too tired to debate you, but I'm not too tired to tell you what makes sense and what doesn't. I suggest you go home and think about what happened tonight and decide."

Stern lifted a brow. "Decide what?"

"Whether or not you want it to happen again. You have to make a decision as to whether you're going to teach JoJo how to become an expert kisser or leave it to someone else."

Stern felt a deep lump in his throat. "Someone else?"

"Yes. You know how women are. They only ask you to do something once, and if you're slow to act they'll get someone else to do it. I haven't been to the Golden Wrench in a while, but I bet JoJo has a number of men working there who would love to teach her how to kiss. And it might not stop there."

The picture Zane had painted in Stern's mind suddenly had his blood boiling. "I'm leaving."

Zane remained seated. "Good night."

"And I won't ever ask you for advice again."

Zane chuckled when he heard his front door slam behind his cousin moments later. He took a sip of his coffee and said, "Yes, you will, Stern. Yes, you will."

"Why are you all smiles today, JoJo?"

JoJo's smile faded as Wanda approached. "You're imagining things. I wasn't smiling." She twisted the wrench to remove the battery from the car she was working on.

"Yes, you were, and I noticed you've been smiling all morning. Something happen last night on your date with Stern?"

JoJo lifted a brow. "It wasn't a date. We merely went to a movie. And who told you about it?"

"You did. Don't you remember?"

In all honesty, she didn't. But there was a possibility that she had absentmindedly mentioned it because it wasn't unusual for her and Stern to go out. "No, I don't remember, but it doesn't matter. This is Wednesday, our busiest day of the week, and I intend for it to be a good day."

"So if it's not Stern putting a smile on your face, it must be because you know that Walter Carmichael is here today."

"Is he?" she asked, wondering why her body wasn't reacting. No increase in her pulse. No deep pounding of her heart. No unsteady breathing.

"Yes, he's in Beeker's bay. He looks good as usual."

"Why is he here? He doesn't have a tune-up for another three thousand miles."

"Something about a tear in the leather seat on the passenger side. I heard him tell Beeker it was caused by the buckle from some woman's boot. He wasn't too happy about it. I guess you should go out and say hello to your soon-to-be Boo."

JoJo wiped the grease from her hands before grabbing her clipboard off her desk. She then smiled over at Wanda. "I think I will."

Moments later, JoJo entered the bay where Beeker stood talking to Walter Carmichael. From Walter's profile she saw similarities between him and Stern. Both were tall, well-dressed and handsome. But that's where the similarities ended. Although Stern wore serious expressions a lot of the time, he had a smile that snuck up on you. Stern's smile would curve the corners of his lips and practically take your breath away. She'd seen Walter Carmichael smile only once and that's when she had complimented him on how well he took care of his car.

Both men glanced up when they saw her and she smiled in greeting. "Hello, Mr. Carmichael. Glad to see you again."

"I wouldn't be here if it wasn't for the tear in my seat," he said, sounding annoyed. "I'm just glad you have a good upholstery team. Beeker assures me the seat can be repaired as good as new."

"Then I'm sure it can be." JoJo knew she wasn't looking her best. She was wearing her work uniform, work shoes and a cap, but still…the man wasn't giving her a sideways glance. She decided not to let it bother her. On Saturday night he would see that she could clean up really nice.

"Well, if you need anything else, let me know. We appreciate our customers."

She really hadn't expected him to say anything in return, but it would have been nice to hear something like… thank you. Instead, he turned back to Beeker and began discussing another car-related issue, dismissing her.

She broke into the conversation, saying, "Well, I've got work to do. Have a good day, Mr. Carmichael."

Instead of responding, he merely nodded, dismissing her again as he continued his conversation with Beeker. Seeing he had no interest in her whatsoever, she left Beeker's bay to return to her own. She'd seen the work log; it would be a long and busy day. She didn't have time to be annoyed with a man who wasn't interested. But she hoped she would get his attention when he saw her Saturday night.

Eight hours later, feeling totally exhausted, she entered her home through the garage. As soon as she reached her bedroom she snatched the cap off her head, stripped off her clothes and headed for the bathroom to take a shower. After that, she would rest up a minute and then throw on something casual before heading out to meet with Pam.

Instead of driving the distance to Westmoreland Country, which was on the outskirts of town, she was meeting Pam in downtown Denver. Pam was going to be in town checking out an empty building she was thinking about purchasing for the acting school she wanted to open. She already had one such school in Wyoming, where she used to live, and she wanted to start another one here in Colorado. She and Pam would have dinner together at Larry's, a café around the corner from the potential school building and a short drive from where JoJo lived.

JoJo had worked on a total of eleven cars today, doing various things, from changing the oil to installing a couple of alternators, and she was bone-tired. She could barely keep her eyes open when she stepped into the shower. However, once the water hit her face she felt more alive. All day she had been too busy to think about that kiss she'd shared with Stern last night, but on the drive home, and now, she couldn't get it out of her mind. Warm sensations flowed through her just thinking about it.

Of course she'd known she lacked knowledge in certain sexual areas, like kissing, but even without a wealth of experience she didn't think it got any better than it had been with Stern. The man's kiss made her body quiver inside. There was no doubt he was an expert. She didn't want to think of the number of women he'd kissed to reach that status. The idea of the many women Stern messed around with had never bothered her before, so why was it bothering her now?

She knew the answer, which was why she'd created this plan in the first place. She needed a diversion, even if that meant going after someone like Walter. She hoped he'd just been having a bad day and that his attitude today wasn't the norm.

After drying herself off, she quickly went to her closet to pick out something to wear and suddenly noted that her wardrobe contained mostly blouses, T-shirts and jeans. She owned a few pairs of slacks and a couple of pantsuits—black, brown and navy. But no dresses. Whenever she had to attend a formal event, like a wedding or a funeral, she wore a pantsuit.

At the hunting lodge, one of Stern's suggestions had been for her to show off her legs. That meant a shopping trip. She would bring that up with Pam when they met.

A part of her was getting excited about all of her plans and the upcoming weekend. In the end, she hoped all of these changes worked out in her favor.

Dillon stuck his head in the door. "You're still here?"

"Come in," Stern called out as he leaned back in his chair. "Yes, I thought I would work late to catch up on a few things. I see that we'll be closing the Harvey deal next week."

"Let's keep our fingers crossed that it really happens this time. Karl Harvey has postponed signing this thing too often to suit me. It will be great if we finally get that tract of land in Minnesota. According to Riley, we already have a potential investor who wants to build a medical complex there."

Stern nodded. "I know why I'm still here at this hour, but what's your excuse? It's almost six o'clock."

Dillon smiled. "I'm meeting Pam later. She came into town to meet with the owners of that warehouse."

"The one she wants to turn into an acting school?"

"Yes, and then later she's meeting with JoJo at Larry's."

Stern raised a brow. "JoJo?"

"Yes," Dillon said, coming into the office, closing the door behind him and taking the chair in front of Stern's desk. "Something about beauty tips or a makeover or something."

Stern tensed at the thought of JoJo moving ahead with her plans. "Dil, can I ask you something?"

"Sure."

"If your best friend asked a favor of you, would you do it?"

Dillon was thoughtful for a minute before he said, "Depends on what the favor is. I won't break the law for anyone."

"It doesn't involve breaking the law."

"Then I'd make sure it wouldn't be immoral, unethical or harmful to anyone. If all that works out then yes, I would do the favor."

Now it was Stern's turn to be thoughtful as he built a steeple with his fingers. "But what if this favor could change the dynamics of your relationship with your best friend?"

Dillon didn't say anything for a long moment. "In that

case, I would think long and hard about whether or not it was what either of us wanted or could handle."

JoJo smiled when she walked into Larry's and saw Pam had already been seated. As always, Pam looked radiant. JoJo could see how Dillon had fallen in love with his wife so quickly.

"I hope you haven't been waiting long," JoJo said as she gave Pam a hug before sliding into the chair across the table.

"Not at all. I took the liberty of indulging in a glass of wine. It's been one of those days."

"Tell me about it," JoJo said, grinning. "I was under the hood of eleven cars too many today."

"But you enjoy your work," Pam said.

"Immensely."

Pam smiled. "And from your phone call I understand there's a man you're trying to impress?"

"Yes." JoJo paused when the waiter came to take her drink order. When he left she said, "I have a good idea where he will be this Saturday night and I want to go there, looking totally different than I do when he sees me at the shop. In other words, I want a grand entrance that will knock off his socks. Can your guy do that?"

When JoJo had talked to Pam yesterday, Pam had said the guy she used as a hairstylist could also do wonders with makeup. He wasn't heavy-handed and applied just enough to reveal a woman's inner beauty.

"Absolutely. Ritz is fabulous and I would love for you to meet him."

Excitement poured through JoJo veins. "I'd like that."

"So you want me to make the appointment?"

"Yes. Please."

Pam beamed. "Consider it done. And you'll probably need a manicure and pedicure. Even a wax."

JoJo tried not to frown as she wondered if Walter Carmichael was worth all the changes she was about to make.

"And what about an outfit?" Pam interrupted her thoughts to ask.

The waiter sat JoJo's glass of wine in front of her. She took a sip. "Stern thinks I should wear a dress."

Pam lifted a brow. "Does he?"

JoJo nodded. "He said I have a great pair of legs and that I don't show them enough."

"Interesting." Pam said, looking at JoJo over her glass of wine.

"In fact, the entire makeover thing was his idea."

"Was it really?" Pam asked.

"Yes."

Pam didn't say anything for a few moments, as if she was giving JoJo's words serious thought. "Well, I'm free on Friday and I'd love to go dress shopping with you. I know just the boutique that might have selections that would interest you. And, if you don't mind, I'd like to ask Chloe to join us. She's sort of a fashion expert."

JoJo knew that to be true. Chloe was married to Ramsey Westmoreland, the oldest of Stern's cousins. Chloe also was editor in chief of a national bestselling woman's magazine. "I think that will be wonderful!"

"Then I'll check to see if she is available. How early can we get started Friday morning?"

JoJo lifted a brow. "Friday morning? I thought it would be something we could squeeze in after I get off work."

Pam shook her head. "I wouldn't advise limiting yourself to those hours. Usually when you're shopping for just the right outfit it can take the entire day."

The entire day? JoJo couldn't imagine such a thing.

"Well, okay. I'll divvy up my work orders with the other guys on Friday so I'm free the whole day."

"That's wonderful!"

JoJo took another sip of her wine. She was starting to wonder if getting a new outfit and a makeover was really wonderful or not.

Five

It was close to nine o'clock when Stern drove out of the parking garage connected to Blue Ridge Land Management. He felt good about the work he'd completed. He had cleared a number of files off his desk and the few cases remaining would be finalized before the week ended.

As he steered his car toward the interstate that would take him to Westmoreland Country, his thoughts shifted to JoJo. Although they didn't indulge in long telephone conversations every day, the norm was for him to call her at least once to see how she was doing. He had deliberately not called her today because the last thing he wanted was for her to bring up their kiss last night—or his offer to help her improve on it.

Stern knew JoJo better than he knew anyone, and he of all people understood the depth of her innocence when it came to men. In all the years he'd known her, she'd only had one crush on someone—Frazier Lewis in the eleventh grade. Frazier had been well-known around school, a popular athlete and ladies' man—and, as far as Stern was concerned, a real jerk.

Frazier had pretended to return JoJo's affections long enough for JoJo to install running boards and state-of-the-art speakers into his truck. But once he'd gotten what he wanted, she hadn't been good enough to be asked to the prom. Frazier had asked Mallory Shivers instead. And if that hadn't been bad enough, Frazier had bragged about how he had used JoJo to help with his truck. Otherwise, he'd said, he would never have given her the time of day. She wasn't his type. She wasn't pretty enough and he'd even called her a grease monkey.

Frazier had ended up regretting his words when Stern whipped his behind after school. To this day, Stern doubted JoJo knew about the butt-whipping he'd given Frazier. Now, he hoped history wasn't about to repeat itself.

She still refused to tell him anything about the guy she was interested in, which made him uncomfortable. The last thing he wanted to deal with was JoJo crying in his arms the way she'd done after Frazier had dumped her.

As far as Stern was concerned, nobody would mistreat JoJo and live to tell about it without feeling some kind of pain. Which was why he was determined to find out this Walter guy's full name and where JoJo planned to hook up with the man this weekend.

Stern shook his head as he merged into traffic on the interstate. Only JoJo would assume that teaching her the fundamentals of kissing would be no different than teaching her how to play checkers. She trusted him and knew he wouldn't take advantage of her. But she didn't fully understand the inner workings of a man's body. Even with the best of intentions, a man could not just *stop* desiring a woman…even when that woman was his best friend.

Stern would admit that he'd been pretty angry when he'd left Zane's house last night, mainly because his cousin had tried pushing unacceptable thoughts into his head. It was only after he'd gotten home, showered and crawled into bed that Stern saw what had really taken place. His cousin hadn't pushed anything into his head. Zane had only tried to get him to admit the thoughts that were already there. Thoughts that had been planted a while ago but hadn't been watered and hadn't sprouted. But somehow they'd now started to grow.

And that was the main reason he couldn't teach JoJo how to kiss. He had *felt* things, and, for a moment, he'd gotten so absorbed in the kiss that he forgot he was kissing JoJo. She'd made him lose his head, which wasn't good.

But even though he didn't want to lose his head with her again, another part of him couldn't forget Zane's warning: if Stern didn't do the teaching, then someone else would. The idea of JoJo locking lips with any other man grated on Stern's insides and sent a shiver of anger up his spine.

He was convinced that sudden spike of emotion was what made him push the button on his steering wheel to connect to his car's operator. "Yes, Mr. Westmoreland?"

"Connect me with Jovonnie Jones."

"Business or residence?"

"Residence."

"Just a moment for the connection."

"Thank you."

It took less than a minute for JoJo's voice to come on the line. Immediately, an unexpected shiver of desire rushed up Stern's spine. He tightened his gut. What the hell was that about?

"Hi, Stern."

"Hi. You're doing okay?"

"Yes. I worked on eleven cars today, came home,

showered then met with Pam for drinks at Larry's. We talked about my makeover."

Yes, he'd heard about that meeting from Dillon. "How did it go?"

"Okay. I have an appointment with Ritz, her hairstylist and makeup artist, on Saturday morning, and she, Chloe and I are going shopping for an outfit the day before, so I won't be in the shop. Can you believe it might take the entire day just to find one outfit?"

Yes, he believed it. He'd hung around the females in his family enough to know about their shopping sprees.

"So what are you doing now?" he asked her.

"Reading a chapter of this book you gave me before going to bed. Why?"

He swallowed deeply. "I worked late tonight and just left the office a few minutes ago," he said, already getting off the exit to go back toward town. "I figured tonight would be a good time to stop by and get you started with Kissing 101. Are you game?"

He heard the catch in her voice when she answered, "Yes, I'm game."

Less than twenty minutes later JoJo heard the sound of Stern's car pulling into her driveway and she drew in a deep breath. A tiny shiver stirred her belly. He'd made this unexpected visit just so she could indulge in Kissing 101.

Ever since she'd hung up the phone she'd tried to convince herself that his visit was no big deal. She needed to improve her kissing and he was willing to show her how it was done. It wouldn't be the first time he had helped her improve a skill. When she'd wanted to be a better water-skier, he had taken her to Gemma Lake. When she had wanted to improve her violin playing, he had assisted her with that.

Upon hearing the sound of Stern's car door closing, she moved toward the front door and opened it just as he walked up the steps to the porch. He smiled and tilted the brim of his Stetson. "You look nice tonight, Jovonnie."

Jovonnie? Look nice? She was still wearing the brown slacks and beige top she'd put on for her meeting with Pam earlier. JoJo figured he must have decided to throw some playacting into her kissing lessons to set the mood. Without saying anything, she stepped back as he entered the house. Something about the look in his eyes gave her pause.

"Stern," she said, trying to fight the lust consuming her. "Thanks. You look nice, too." She moved toward the center of her living room.

He closed the door behind him and walked toward her with movements that were so full of virility she felt weak in the knees. And when he came to a stop with only one inch keeping their bodies from touching, she realized she was attracted to him more than ever before. He was tall and handsome, with a beautifully proportioned body that would make any woman take notice.

The outline of his body strained against the fabric of his dark jacket and emphasized the width of his shoulders. The denim jeans covered his long muscular legs and rounded off what she considered a powerfully sexy male physique.

He cupped her face in his hands and whispered in a deep, husky voice, "Have I told you lately just how utterly beautiful you are?"

Utterly beautiful? She dismissed his words, trying to remember they were playacting. Even so, as she looked into the darkness of his eyes, she heard herself saying, "No, not lately."

He smiled and the way his lips curved made a deep yearning spread all through her stomach. "Definitely an error on my part," he said huskily. "One that I need to correct immediately." Then he lowered his mouth to hers.

He didn't take her mouth right away like he had the last time. Instead, he hovered over her mouth as if to allow her to absorb his heated breath into her own. Then he leaned in closer and slowly slid his tongue between her parted lips.

On instinct, her own tongue was there to meet his and they began a dance that had fire rushing through her body. She closed her eyes as the sensations became almost unbearable.

The kiss intensified. He locked their lips in a way that made hers a willing captive to his. He greedily feasted on her mouth, causing her to moan deep within her throat. This kiss was deeper, more thorough and more arousing than the other one had been, though she wasn't sure how that could be possible. How could a kiss meant for teaching be so convincingly arousing?

All too soon he released her chin and dropped his hands. She slowly opened her eyes and looked at him. As he tried catching his breath, she tried doing the same. Even as he drew in deep gulps of air he gazed at her with a seductive look. She couldn't help wondering how he'd been able to play his role so well.

"So," she said, finally finding her voice. "How do you think I did just now?"

The look of obvious approval in his eyes pleased her. "Very well," he said softly as his eyes raked boldly over her.

It was then that she had to remind herself that the look

in his eyes was only a part of his role-playing. The person who'd just kissed her was her best friend—Stern—and the kiss hadn't been a real kiss at all but a lesson. But it had been some lesson!

He reached out and took her hand in his. "Come on, let's sit down on the sofa and talk about it."

She lifted a brow. "Talk about it?"

He nodded. "We need to cover every aspect of that kiss in full detail."

She swallowed tightly, thinking, *Oh, boy.*

Stern sat down on the sofa and gathered JoJo to his side, not ready to let her get too far away just yet. The kiss that had been meant as a learning lesson for her had overwhelmed him, making him fully aware of just what power JoJo packed and how easy it might be for a man to take advantage of her vulnerability.

His reaction to the kiss had been quick and magnetic—and that really wasn't supposed to happen. He was supposed to remain aloof, detached and indifferent. Definitely disengaged.

But he'd gotten engaged, connected and way too involved.

"Well?"

He saw her watching him expectantly. Turning to her, he continued to hold her hand. If she found it odd, she said nothing about it. It seemed her focus was on what he had to say.

"First of all," he started off, "my approach tonight was one of setting the mood. You should have picked up on what my intentions were the moment I arrived."

She nodded. "I did. I saw that look in your eyes and noted your body language and knew you had gone into playacting mode."

He wondered what she would think if she knew he hadn't been acting. When she'd opened the door and he'd seen her standing there, his reaction to her had been purely sensual and definitely real.

"To start things off," he said, "I gave you a compliment about how nice you looked. That was intended to soften you up, make you mellow. That should have been another hint at my intentions. However, there shouldn't have been any doubt in your mind what I intended to do when I cupped your face."

She nodded. "There wasn't."

"Good. That kiss was one I classify as an *I like you* kiss. A French kiss between two people wanting to know each other better. Not too light and not too heavy."

"Do you think that's the type Walter will use?"

Stern flinched at the thought of the man kissing her using any method. "More than likely, if he's a smooth sort of guy," he said, forcing the words from his mouth. "If he tries rushing things, then he'll use one of those *I want you* kisses. Those can be dangerous."

"In what way?"

"Those are intended to make a woman lose her head because the man has only one thing on his mind—getting you into the nearest bed."

"Oh," she said.

He watched her nibble at her bottom lip and knew she was thinking about what he'd said.

"So what should I do if he gives me that kind of kiss and I'm not ready for it?"

"End it immediately," he said with more force than necessary. "A woman can end a kiss at any time, especially if she thinks it's aggressive or if it's more than what she's ready for."

"Okay," she said, nodding. "Let's try one."

He raised a brow. "Excuse me?"

"I said, let's try one of those. I need to make sure I can tell the difference between an *I like you* kiss and an *I want you* kiss."

Grinning, he said, "Trust me, you'll be able to tell the difference, JoJo."

"I want to be sure."

He stared at her, certain she had no idea what she was asking of him. "I don't think it's a good idea."

"Why? It's me, Stern. JoJo. I'm the last person you would want to take to bed, but for this kiss I need you to pretend so I can know the difference. I want Walter to like me, but I'm not ready to sleep with him."

Stern sighed deeply, glad to hear that.

"But I don't want him to catch me with my guard down. What if I return the kiss not knowing what kind it is? That wouldn't be fair to him and he might think I'm a tease."

Stern didn't give a royal damn what this Walter guy thought. And he had to bite his tongue not to tell JoJo that very thing. She was trying to impress a man who might not deserve all the trouble she was going through.

"Stern?"

He looked at her and saw the pleading in her eyes. She actually didn't know the power of such a kiss, much less where it could lead. Maybe he should make sure she did. "Okay, JoJo, but only because you asked."

He stood, removed his jacket and placed it across the back of the sofa before sitting back down. "Remember, with *any* kiss you can pull back at any time."

"What if I pull back and the guy doesn't stop and keeps kissing me anyway?"

"Then you slap the hell out of him."

She smiled. "Okay."

He returned her smile, knowing she wouldn't hesitate to do so. "All right, let's get started. Be prepared because there's an intense degree of French kissing in this sort of kiss. Just thought I'd warn you."

"All right."

He leaned toward her. She smelled good, and whether she knew it or not, she exuded a heavy dose of femininity just the way she was. She had her hair in a ponytail, didn't have on any makeup and was wearing slacks and a blouse. Although he'd been the one to suggest a makeover, he wasn't sure whether one would suit her. She was JoJo, and as far as he was concerned, she had an inner beauty that was an innate part of her no matter what she was wearing on the outside.

"Stern?"

It was only then that he realized he'd been sitting there staring at her. "Yes?"

"Is something wrong?"

He could come clean now and tell her that yes, something was wrong—he just didn't know what. He could also tell her he didn't want this Walter guy to come within five feet of her, but if she asked why, he wouldn't know what to tell her other than *just because.*

"No, nothing's wrong. I'm just trying to figure out why someone as beautiful as you are doesn't have men constantly knocking at your door." He pulled the band off her hair and then wound his hands into the dark strands.

She rolled her eyes. "Role-playing again?"

"Yes…" *If that's what she wants to believe…*

"Then I guess I need to get into the act, too," she said, placing the pad of a finger into the dimple in his chin. She'd done that before but her doing it now had his flesh zinging.

"I like this dimple right here," she said, smiling.

"Apparently," he said, trying to control the way her touch was making him feel. "Just like I have a thing for your hair."

"Do you?"

"You know I do. I'm not very fond of your cap."

She chuckled. "But you know why I wear it. Can't have hair falling in my face while changing a battery." She thought for a minute. "I think my profession turns off most men."

"And I can see how it can turn some men on."

She lifted a brow. "Really? How?"

"A woman who can change spark plugs and a tire in record time and doesn't need a man to install brake pads has to be dynamite in every other facet of her life."

"I like that theory of yours."

"And I like you." Stern felt a web of desire building between them and knew it wasn't pretense. It was the real thing. Suddenly, he reached out and swept her from her spot on the sofa and into his lap, ignoring her surprised gasp. Before she could skim out of his grasp, he placed his arms around her.

"Now," he said huskily, "this is where I want you for the time being. Do you have a problem with it?"

She stared down at him for a long moment before saying, "No, I don't have a problem with it."

A part of JoJo wondered whether or not she should have problems with this scenario. Stern had no idea of her feelings for him, of how she constantly fought them. He had no clue that it was his face that invaded her dreams at night, that it was his lips she fantasized about kissing. He had no idea how much she *wanted* his kisses. This role-playing was kind of fun. She could let herself go, let herself enjoy the attraction she felt for him without him knowing the truth.

"JoJo?"

Was she mistaken or had his eyes gotten darker? She must be mistaken. "Yes?"

"We can decide not to do this and call it a night."

Was that reluctance she heard in his voice? "No, I'm good. I want to do this, Stern. I need to do this."

More than you could ever know.

He stared down at her, and then he asked, "Does this Walter mean that much to you?"

She thought about his question. It was on the tip of her tongue to say that no, Walter didn't mean that much to her, Stern did. She wanted to say that she was only using Walter to make her forget about Stern. Instead, she said, "I don't know the answer to that. All I know is that I want him to notice me. To take me seriously. I want him to see me as someone other than the mechanic who keeps his car in check."

"Well, I'm going to be plenty angry if I find out he doesn't appreciate you and the beautiful person that you are. And I'm not saying that as your best friend—I'm saying that as a man who has dated a lot of women and can recognize a gem when he sees it."

His words filled her. No reply could come out. She felt tears trying to gather at the backs of her eyes. Why did he have to go and say such sweet things to her? Words that would give any woman pause and make her long for a man like him?

"Thank you," she finally said when she was capable of speaking.

"Don't ever thank me for any compliments I give you, JoJo, because I mean them."

JoJo bit her lower lip to keep it from trembling as her

heart pounded in her chest. She wished he wouldn't play his role so well. It only made her wish even more that they could move beyond being best friends. Unfortunately, that would never happen. They were best friends and that was all they could ever be to each other.

But, for a short while, as he educated her in the fine art of kissing, she could pretend—and boy would she pretend. "Kiss me, Stern."

He fanned her face with his heated breath as he eased his mouth closer to hers. "Asking a man to kiss you in a voice like that can be dangerous. He'll think he's already won half the battle."

At that moment, she didn't care and to prove she didn't, she placed her arms around his neck. In one smooth, forward motion she leaned up and tilted her mouth to his, blatantly inviting him to do just what she'd asked.

He took her lips in slowly and leisurely, as if he had all the time in the world and intended to make sure she felt every demand he was making on her mouth. He tightened his arms around her and took her mouth with a greed that had her head spinning. This kiss was definitely different from the other two. Its intensity made a moan escape her lips. As he continued to enjoy tasting her, she settled back against his chest, sinking deeply into his warm embrace.

If the purpose of this kind of kiss was to make a woman willing and ready for the bedroom, then she could see it happening…but not with Walter. She doubted she could get into a kiss like this with him. In fact, a kiss like this from him just might turn her off because she would be pretending he was someone else. She would imagine Stern as the man holding her in his arms, as he was doing this very minute. Stern was the man using his lips and tongue to send warm shivers through her.

She wasn't certain who shifted first, but her back was

suddenly pressed against the sofa cushions and she was no longer in Stern's lap. She was lying on the sofa with him over her.

He hadn't let up with his attention to her mouth and he hadn't let go of her. The hunger in his kiss was building a passion in her she'd never experienced before. The kiss had started off slow and drugging. Now it was fiery and hot, sending ecstasy spiraling within her, nearly robbing her of all conscious thought.

But she knew the exact moment when he began unbuttoning her blouse, and she moaned when air touched her chest. Then his hands were there, rubbing against the material of her bra and—

Her cell phone rang and Stern jerked away from her as if he'd been burned. He almost tumbled over in his quickness to get off the sofa. She eased up into a sitting position and, after buttoning her blouse, she picked up the phone off the coffee table. It was a cousin calling her from Detroit and she let it go to voice mail.

"Why didn't you stop me?" Stern asked, seeming to barely get the words out. He had a fierce expression on his face.

She shrugged before saying, "Because I liked it," she told him honestly.

He stared at her for a second before grabbing his jacket off the back of the chair. Angry eyes pinned her when he said, "Not sure these kissing lessons were a good idea. I'll call you sometime tomorrow."

By the time she was on her feet, he was already out the door and had slammed it shut behind him.

Six

The next day Stern paced his office in a bad mood. He was glad Dillon hadn't called any meetings today and that he mostly had the office to himself. Riley was out for the rest of the week because he and Alpha had flown to Daytona to visit her parents. Canyon had taken off at lunch to meet with Keisha and go shopping for a swing set for their son, Beau.

Stern stopped in the middle of the floor and rubbed his hand down his face. He hadn't called JoJo like he'd told her he would, and he didn't plan to do so until he pulled himself together. That kiss last night still had him reeling in a way no kiss ever had before.

He let out a deep sigh. It wasn't as if they were lovers. Far from it. They were best friends who'd agreed to study Kissing 101. The prior kisses with her had left him believing he'd probably imagined their impact. But after last night he knew his imagination wasn't responsible. That kiss, the one that was supposed to be the *I want you* kiss, had done just that—it had left him wanting her with a vengeance. That's why he was so angry and annoyed with himself. She trusted him in a way she trusted no other man and last night he had violated that trust. He had been two seconds away from stripping her naked.

He drew in a deep breath when his cell phone went off and he recognized JoJo's ring tone. He wasn't ready to talk to her yet. He needed time to come to terms with last night. To her, it might have been a kissing lesson, but to him it had been more.

Now, what was he going to do about it?

When she woke up Friday morning JoJo was convinced Stern was avoiding her. She'd called him yesterday to make sure things were okay after he'd stormed out of her place Wednesday night. But he hadn't returned her call. Usually, even if he was in a meeting when she called, he would call her back at the first opportunity. But he hadn't this time.

Sliding out of bed, she headed for the bathroom to shower and dress. She was to meet Pam and Chloe at the Cherry Creek Mall when the doors opened at ten. That would give her time to stop by the coffee shop to grab coffee and a bagel. Hopefully by the time she met Pam and Chloe she would have her head together. At the moment it was still all messed up.

Shaking off the glum knowledge that she was losing her best friend, she stripped and stepped into the shower. Over the past thirty-six hours she had replayed what had happened over and over in her mind. Stern had readied her for the kiss by telling her what kind it would be. She had been prepared. Sort of. She doubted any woman would have been fully prepared for a Stern Westmoreland kiss. It had knocked her off her rocker, but that hadn't been what surprised her.

What she couldn't figure out was Stern's attitude. Had

she gotten more involved in the kiss than he had wanted? Enjoyed it too much? Had she not followed some unwritten script? Had she not ended the kiss when he felt she should have? Was she wrong in suggesting that he help her improve her kissing in the first place?

There was a lot about men that JoJo didn't know, but things had been going great in her life until she'd developed these crazy feelings for Stern that had escalated into love. Now she was trying like heck to rectify the problem by finding someone else to love. Under no circumstances could Stern ever find out how she felt about him. And if that meant no more Kissing 101, well…she'd deal with that decision when she came to it.

A few hours later she placed a smile on her face and joined the two ladies standing in front of the entrance to the mall. Even at ten in the morning both of them looked radiant, beautiful and classy. JoJo would just love looking like that any time of the day. But she had to be realistic. Her job required that she *didn't* look like that. However, she wanted tips on how to present herself in a better light when she went out. She would be celebrating her thirtieth birthday in less than a year. It was time she made some changes.

Giving the two women hugs, JoJo told them how glad she was to see them and how much she appreciated their help. Then, after telling her how much they enjoyed having a chance to help her, Pam and Chloe pulled her toward the first dress shop.

Stern glanced up when he heard the knock on his office door. "Come in."

When the door opened and Zane walked in Stern placed his pen down and leaned back in his chair in surprise. "What brings you out of Westmoreland Country in the middle of the day?"

Zane, his cousin Derringer and Stern's brother Jason were partners in a horse breeding and training company along with various other cousins in Montana and Texas.

"I had to come to town to meet with a potential client. I think we've made another sale," Zane said, sliding his muscular frame into the chair across from Stern's desk. "Since I was out this way I figured I'd check on you."

"Why?" Stern asked, reaching for a couple of paper clips and then tossing them back on his desk.

"Because the last time we talked you seemed rather frustrated."

If truth be told, he was still frustrated, even more so. He would admit to being overwhelmed by the events of the past few days. There was no doubt in his mind that JoJo was wondering why he hadn't returned her call from yesterday. He'd never done that before.

"The situation with JoJo has worsened," he said in an exasperated tone.

Zane straightened in his chair with a concerned expression on his face. "How so?"

"I decided to do the kissing lesson as you suggested. However, I almost lost control, Zane. You were right. When I was kissing her, I didn't see her as my best friend, but as a potential lover."

"And you still have a problem with that? I'm sure there are several situations where best friends become lovers, Stern. People change. Feelings change. Relationships change. Your feelings for her probably have been shifting for a while now without you even realizing they were doing so."

Stern frowned. "But you know how I am when it comes to women, Zane. I date them and don't give them another thought. Some I take out more than once or twice, but that's seldom. And the thought of a lasting relationship with any of them never crosses my mind. I couldn't treat JoJo that way."

"No, you couldn't and you wouldn't. She means too much to you, which brings up another issue."

"What?"

"When are you going to admit to yourself that you're falling in love with her?"

Stern looked stunned. Then he looked indignant. "What are you talking about? I am not falling in love with her."

"Are you sure about that? I almost lost Channing because I refused to acknowledge I had feelings for her. I think if there's any possibility you might be falling for JoJo, you're doing her a disservice not to let her know. And you need to do it before it's too late."

Stern pushed away from his desk, stood and moved over to the window. He thought of everything that had transpired since the week he and JoJo had spent at the lodge, when she'd first brought up the fact that she was interested in a man. He didn't have to think hard to recall his emotions, his anxieties and his fears. Could they have been based on the fact that he had hidden feelings for her? Feelings he'd had for a while, possibly for years, tucked deep inside?

He turned back to Zane. "It's already too late. She's set her sights on someone else, remember? This Walter guy."

"So? Is that supposed to mean something?"

Stern sighed and shook his head. Sometimes he wondered about Zane and all the wisdom he was supposed to have bottled inside that Westmoreland brain of his. "It would mean something to most people, I would think."

Zane shrugged his massive shoulders. "Not to a Westmoreland, not when he wants something bad enough. It's up to you to determine, first, if you're falling for JoJo, and if you are, what you're going to do about it. If you want to lose her to another man, then that's your business. But if it were me, I wouldn't give up my woman without a fight."

Stern rolled his eyes. "First of all, she's not my woman. All JoJo feels for me is friendship, Zane, regardless of whether I'm falling for her or not."

Zane stood. "Then if I were you, I'd give this Walter guy a damn good run for his money. And I would definitely start letting JoJo know how I feel. You might be surprised. You might discover she feels the same way. I've said for years that the two of you had a strange relationship. Best friends or not, you are in each other's pockets."

Stern released a deep breath. As far as he was concerned, nobody had been in each other's pockets more than his cousin Bane and his longtime girlfriend Crystal, and look what had happened to them…but that had been years ago and was another story. "I'll give your advice some consideration," he said.

Zane chuckled as he headed for the door. "Yeah, you do that. It's time for you to think like a Westmoreland."

JoJo bit her bottom lip as she looked at all the dresses Pam and Chloe were holding up. She was convinced she had checked out more than a hundred today and it wasn't even two o'clock yet.

"Well, which ones do you like?" Stern's cousin Megan, who was a doctor of anesthesiology, had joined them when they'd taken a break for lunch. It didn't take long for JoJo to discover that Megan enjoyed shopping just as much as Pam and Chloe did.

Which *ones* and not just which *one?* Jeez, she'd already purchased six dresses. In addition to the one she planned to wear tomorrow night, the ladies said she would need additional outfits for all her other dates with Walter. They had more faith in her ability to nab his interest than she did. "I like the yellow one and the multicolored one," she said.

Megan beamed. "Good choices. Those were my favorites, too." And Pam and Chloe nodded their approval. Frankly, she'd liked all the outfits she'd purchased today and she had looked good in them.

"After we get these paid for, then we need to visit Sandra's Lingerie Boutique. We've taken care of the outerwear, so now it's on to the underwear," Pam said, smiling.

JoJo thought she had plenty of underwear back home in the top drawer of her dresser, but the three women had stressed earlier that she needed something new and sexy. Honestly, she didn't know why. Even if she and Walter hit it off, there was no way she would sleep with him the first night. Nor the second. Or the third. She might be interested in Walter, but that interest had its limits when it came to sex.

"That was Lucia," Chloe said, sliding her mobile phone back into her purse. "She thought it would be fun to let our guys babysit tonight while we have a girls' night out dinner with JoJo after our day of shopping. So she, Bella, Keisha and Kalina will join us for dinner at McKays."

JoJo thought that was a great idea. She had known Megan, Gemma and Bailey all her life, and because she was best friends with Stern she also had gotten to know the women his brothers and cousins had married.

A half hour later she was in Sandra's Lingerie Boutique looking at undies. Never had she seen so many shapes, sizes and colors. She would have to admit she was drawn to the matching sets. There was just something special about wearing a bra that was the same color as your panties.

"Okay, are you a thong, briefs, bikini or hip-hugger kind of girl?" Pam asked as they moved around the display looking for her size.

"Excuse me?"

Pam smiled. "Here, I'll show you." She held up each type for JoJo.

"I'm a briefs girl," JoJo said now that she had a clearer understanding of the question.

"Um, not tomorrow night," Chloe said, holding up a thong. "This is what you're going to need with the dress you selected."

JoJo gazed at the itsy-bitsy scrap of almost nothing and thought...*seriously?*

"You don't want any panty lines to show," Megan explained.

"Oh." She didn't worry about such things when she wore jeans.

"And we plan to be there tomorrow when you get dressed," Chloe announced.

JoJo blinked. "You do?"

"Of course. We want you to knock your guy off his feet."

After having spent almost the entire day going from store to store and trying on dress after dress, she certainly hoped she would knock Walter off his feet. Absently, she pulled the phone out of her purse to see if she'd missed any calls...specifically, any calls from Stern. She fought back a feeling of disappointment when she saw that he hadn't called.

"Any ideas on your hairstyle, JoJo?" Chloe asked, interrupting her thoughts. "I understand Ritz is taking care of your hair and makeup, and he's good."

"That's what I hear," JoJo said, checking out matching bras.

"Are you going to get it cut?"

JoJo glanced over at Pam. "No, Stern likes it long."

"Stern?" Megan asked, frowning. "Who cares what Stern likes? He's not the one you're trying to impress."

As JoJo continued to pick out matching panties and bra sets, she thought Megan had a point. But still…

Think like a Westmoreland…

Zane's words flowed through Stern's mind as he locked up his desk and prepared to leave the office later that day. How should a man who was used to being pursued switch focus and become the pursuer? It would definitely be one hell of a game changer.

He stood just as his cell phone went off. He checked his caller ID and saw it was Dillon. "Yes, Dil?"

"I'm just giving everyone a head's-up. There's been a change in tonight's chow down."

It was customary for the Westmorelands to get together on Friday nights for dinner. "What's the change?"

"The men are doing the cooking since our ladies decided to take JoJo out to dinner after her long day of shopping."

"Oh."

"To keep things simple, I'm asking every man to bring their specialty. Since you don't have one, you can drop by the bakery on your way home and pick up something for dessert."

"That will work."

"And Stern?"

"Yes?"

"Those of us with kids are babysitting, which means they eat what we eat, so don't buy a rum cake."

Stern chuckled. Everyone knew rum cake was his favorite. "Gotcha."

After hanging up with Dillon, Stern sat back down in his chair. *Think like a Westmoreland.* A few minutes later he glanced at his watch. Smiling, he pulled his cell phone from his jacket and punched in a few numbers.

"The Golden Wrench Automotive Repair Shop. This is Wanda. How may I help you?"

"Hi, beautiful. This is Stern. And you can help me by giving me some information I have a feeling you know."

Seven

JoJo stepped out of her bedroom, walked into her living room and was met by a chorus of collective gasps.

"JoJo, you look stunning."

"Sensational."

"Hot."

"You don't even look like the same person."

JoJo smiled at the women staring at her. "Thanks. I feel like all those things tonight," she said, glancing down at herself.

She looked back up at the ladies who filled her living room. "I want to thank all of you for your help. Not only for shopping with me yesterday and being there for the hair and makeover today, but just being here for me now. Giving me the confidence to pull this off."

There was no need to tell them that the one other person she wanted here with her, the one person she needed to give her a confidence boost and his blessing, was her best friend. But Stern wasn't here and she hadn't heard from him since Wednesday. His actions had pretty much let her know things were no longer the same between them. His reaction angered her every time she thought about it. It had been his idea for the makeover. And he had kissed her first! Was it wrong for her to want to improve her kissing skills?

"I went online and checked out your Walter," Bailey Westmoreland broke into JoJo's thoughts to say. "He's a cutie, but his profile picture makes him look like a stuffed shirt in that business suit. Are you sure he frequents a place like the Punch Bowl? That used to be Derringer and Riley's hangout. For a long time we thought they had purchased stock in the place."

"It would be just my luck if tonight is the one night he changes his mind and stays home or goes someplace else," JoJo said, hoping that wouldn't be the case.

"Then it will be his loss," Pam said, smiling. "But I have a feeling this is going to be your lucky night."

JoJo drew in a deep breath. She hoped so. Glancing down at her hands she remembered how Ritz had fussed about how awful they looked and how many wonders he'd had to pull off to make them look presentable. Her nails were painted a pretty shade of pink, which looked good with the multiple colors in her dress.

"And I'm glad you didn't cut your hair after all," Chloe said. "The way Ritz has it styled makes it look fuller around your face. I can't say enough just how gorgeous you look."

And if it never happened again in her life, at least for tonight she felt gorgeous. She looked at her watch. "Well, it's time for me to leave. I want to thank all of you again for tonight and yesterday. Because of you, I feel special."

"You are special," Megan said, smiling. "And before you leave I want to take plenty of pictures. I can't wait to show Rico how beautiful you look."

* * *

"Thanks for letting me perform here tonight, Sampson."

The older man, who had prepared Stern's mother for her first piano recital at age eight, looked up from the piano and smiled. "My pleasure, Stern. Once in a while I was able to talk Riley into sitting on this bench and whenever he did, the crowd would go wild. Your mom made sure all her boys had an ear for music."

Stern nodded. His mom had made certain all seven of her sons loved music as much as she did. Dillon and Micah mastered guitar; Riley and Bane, the piano; Canyon the French horn and Stern the violin. After his parents' death, Dillon made sure they continued developing their love for music by calling on Sampson to give them lessons.

"Riley much preferred being in the audience surrounded by the beautiful ladies vying for his attention." Sampson shook his head. "It's hard for me to believe lover boy is getting married at the end of the month."

"You, me and a number of others," Stern said, grinning. "But once you meet Alpha you'll understand."

Sampson glanced at his watch. "The show starts at eight, but if you want you can go out front and enjoy yourself for a while. Just tell Sweety to put any of your drinks on my tab."

"Thanks, but I'll hang back here until showtime." Stern decided not to mention that sitting on the stool backstage by the observation window gave him a good view of the customers without them knowing they were being watched. His cousin Ian had a similar setup at his casino in Lake Tahoe.

"But you can tell me something," Stern added.

Sampson looked over at him. "What?"

"Walter Carmichael. I understand he comes here a lot. Is he here tonight?"

Sampson leaned up and strained his neck over the piano to look out through the glass. "Yes. He's here. You know him?"

Detecting Sampson's disapproving tone, Stern met the older man's gaze. "No, I don't know him but someone mentioned this is his hangout on the weekends."

"It is most of the time, unfortunately. He has lots of money and likes throwing it around to impress the women. Some he can impress, and others he can't. He gets annoyed quickly with those he can't. I think he feels entitled to any woman he wants. And I hear he has a mean streak. A few months ago, he tried roughing up one of the ladies when she refused his advances. It didn't happen here—otherwise Sweety wouldn't let him come back. I understand they met here but then he took her out on a date a few weeks later. Rumor has it that his daddy paid the woman a lot of money to drop the charges."

"His daddy?"

"Yes. Carmichael's from the Midwest and his family is pretty well off, which is why he drives that flashy car and wears expensive clothes. I understand he only works because his father decreased his allowance a couple years ago, although he's been known to boast that his mother sends him money on the side. I also heard he's in Denver because he had to flee from Indiana amid a scandal involving a married woman whose husband threatened to kill him." Sampson lifted a brow. "Anything else you want to know?"

Stern had heard enough. From the rundown Sampson had just given him, there was no way he would let someone of Carmichael's character become involved with

JoJo. "Yes, there is something else. I need you to point him out to me."

If his request seemed odd, Sampson gave no sign of it. He looked through the one-way glass and Stern followed the direction of his gaze. "That's him in the navy blue slacks and tan jacket, looking like he just stepped off the page of one of those fancy magazines."

Stern studied the man's features. He was hanging with a group of guys at the bar, laughing at something one of them had said. Stern decided then and there that he didn't like the guy. Sampson was right; Carmichael had the look of rich-boy entitlement written all over him.

Stern was about to turn around to say as much to Sampson when he noticed Carmichael, his friends and several other men in the Punch Bowl look toward the entrance of the club. Stern's gaze shifted to see what had snagged everyone's attention. His eyes widened and the breath was snatched from his lungs. Wow! Holy…

It was JoJo. And she looked absolutely, positively hot. Damn, what had she done to herself? Her hair was fluffed up on her head in a style that showcased the beauty of her face. Her face was perfectly made up and not overdone. Her lashes appeared longer, her cheeks a little rosy and her lips a luscious ruby-red.

And then there was what had to be the sexiest dress he'd ever seen. The hem was shorter in the front, barely covering her thighs, with the skirt only a little longer in the back, showing off her gorgeous legs in a pair of blue stilettoes. And the plunging neckline supported firm breasts that made him wonder if she was even wearing a bra.

"Nice-looking lady," he heard Sampson say. "I hope she knows what she's doing by coming here looking that hot without a date. The hungry wolves are certainly out tonight. Look."

Stern switched his gaze from JoJo to the crowd. Every man in the place had eyes on her. Some were even licking their lips. Stern felt his blood pressure shoot sky-high.

He saw the moment she noticed Carmichael and smiled at him. But Stern knew JoJo better than anyone and he could tell by the way her bottom lip quivered beneath that smile that she wasn't as confident as she appeared to be.

"This room is soundproof if you need more practice time," he heard Sampson say.

"No, I don't need any more practice time," he replied, not taking his eyes off JoJo. "I'll be ready to do what I need to do when the time comes."

Unknown to Sampson, Stern's response had double meaning. As far as Stern was concerned, tonight he would be squashing any plans JoJo had for her and Carmichael.

JoJo slowly drew in a breath as the hostess led her to a table. When she'd entered, the first set of eyes she'd met had been Walter's, but he didn't seem to recognize her. Granted she looked very different without her uniform, work shoes and cap, but surely something about her would be familiar.

"The show starts in half an hour." The young woman whose name tag read Melissa smiled. "Would you like some wine?"

"Yes, a glass of Moscato."

"Good choice. I'll be back in a minute."

While waiting for the hostess to return with her drink, JoJo forced herself not to glance back over at the men standing at the bar. She'd made eye contact with most of them when she'd first walked in and she didn't want to give them the impression that she was hungry for anyone's company...anyone other than Walter, that is. What if another guy approached her before he did? She would have to turn him down nicely and let him know she wasn't interested. But if that happened and then Walter finally did approach would he feel like the one who'd grabbed the golden ring? Would he feel entitled to whatever he wanted?

"Excuse me. This might sound like a pickup line, but I have a feeling we've met before."

It was Walter. He was smiling down at her in a way that made his lips crinkle at the corners and his eyes sparkle with intense interest. She was relieved he was the first one to approach her. He looked good tonight, but for the life of her, she couldn't recall why she and Wanda had ever thought he favored over Stern. Stern had him beat in the looks department hands down.

She returned his smile, thinking that the night was already going just as she wanted. "We have met, Walter," she said, deciding not to play coy.

She could tell he was surprised and pleased that she knew his name. "Really? It must only have been in passing. There's no way I would have held a conversation with you and not remembered."

He was smooth, but he would have to try a lot harder to truly impress her. She was best friends with the master of lines, and she'd heard Stern use them often enough.

Which reminded her that she hadn't heard from Stern since Wednesday, and he had refused to return her calls. JoJo knew he wasn't sick because none of his cousins had mentioned him being under the weather. That could only mean he was still upset and taking it to a ridiculous level by refusing to talk to her. The only other time they had stopped speaking to each other was in the tenth grade when he'd sworn that she'd deliberately given him chicken pox...like she would deliberately do such a thing. She'd contracted it first and he had caught it within days—right before he was supposed to compete at a band fair.

To keep his siblings and cousins from catching it, which would have meant bad news for Dillon and Ramsey, her father had invited Stern to stay with them while he was recovering. Her father had figured if he had to tolerate one sick and demanding child with the pox he might as well tolerate two. By the end of the second week, Stern had realized she was blameless for his condition and that being sick hadn't been so bad anyway, especially because her father had given him tons of car magazines to read. In fact, if she remembered correctly, he hadn't wanted to leave her house when his time was up. He'd claimed he'd had more fun being sick at her place than being well at his.

Drawing in a deep breath, she forced thoughts of Stern from her mind. The whole point of tonight was to forget about her feelings for him. It wasn't fair to keep comparing Walter to her best friend.

"So where have we met?" Walter asked.

She held his gaze, wanting to read his expression when she told him who she was. "My shop."

He lifted a brow. "Your shop? And just what kind of shop do you have?" He shoved his hands into his pockets and stood in what some women would probably think was a sexy pose.

A smile spread across her lips. "I just saw you this week. I'm surprised you didn't recognize me right away. My name is Jovonnie Jones, from the Golden Wrench. JoJo."

She saw the shocked look in his eyes and it lingered way too long to suit her. What he did next really got to her. He reached out, picked up her hand and checked her nails. What exactly did he expect to find? Grease on her fingertips? Annoyed, she pulled her hand out of his. "Is anything wrong?"

He shook his head as if he was trying to come to terms with what he'd just discovered. "No, I just can't believe you're the same woman who…who…"

It seemed he was having a hard time filling in the blanks, so she said, "The same woman who repairs cars? Always wears a uniform? Puts her hair under a cap?"

"Yes," he said, grinning. "All those things. You clean up rather nicely," he said, his tone dropping as he looked her up and down. "I never would have thought."

Cleaned up rather nicely? Did he assume he was giving her a compliment? The thought made her even more annoyed, but she tried pushing away her aggravation. She had to remember he served a purpose in her life. Little did he know he was making it harder and harder to believe that he could be the one to make her forget about her feelings for Stern.

"Here's your drink," the waitress said, placing the glass of wine in front of her.

"Thanks."

"Are you expecting someone to join you?" Walter asked.

She glanced up at him, tempted to lie outright and say that she was. But she quickly reminded herself that he was the reason she was here tonight. He was the reason she had spent an entire day shopping till she dropped. And today, because of him, she had gotten plucked, waxed and trimmed.

"No, I'm not expecting anyone. I'm here alone."

"I'm here alone, too," he said in a deep, husky tone. "Mind if I join you?"

She forced a smile. "No, I don't mind."

"You okay, son?"

"Yes, I'm okay."

Stern had been so focused on the interactions between JoJo and Carmichael that he'd forgotten Sampson was still in the room. Now Carmichael was sitting at JoJo's table, engaging her in conversation that had her smiling. A player like Stern could easily recognize player instincts in another man, and there was no doubt in his mind that Carmichael was laying it on thick. Now he was pouring more wine into JoJo's glass, and Stern couldn't help wondering if the man's play was to get her drunk. Stern chuckled. If that was Carmichael's plan, he'd better come up with another one because JoJo's body was resistant to alcohol. It was as if the stuff didn't affect her.

"Show's about to start so I'm leaving to open."

Stern glanced over his shoulder. "Okay. And again, thanks for adding my number to tonight's lineup."

"No problem. I figure there's a reason you called last night wanting to perform." Sampson looked past Stern and through the glass to the table where JoJo sat. He then looked at Stern. "Now I know."

Stern swallowed. "Do you?"

"Yes. When a man loves a woman it's hard to keep certain feelings hidden."

Stern frowned. "It's not like that. She and I are just good friends. We're best friends."

"I see."

Was Sampson seeing him in the same way Zane had? That possibility didn't sit well with Stern because he couldn't see what they were seeing. He was glad when

the older man opened the door and left. It kept him from having to say anything more.

Stern leaned back on the stool, bracing his back against the wall as he remembered how fast things had moved yesterday. He didn't have to pump Wanda for information; she'd given it willingly. And once he'd gotten it, setting up his own plan had been easy.

This place used to be Riley and Derringer's favorite hangout and Derringer had called it "pickup alley." Basically, women came here alone to meet men, so this was where men had a tendency to hang out to meet those women. It stood to reason this is where Carmichael would be on the weekends. And the live entertainment was probably the best in Denver, with Sampson on the piano and Mavis on bass.

Stern had come up with the idea of performing, playing his violin, and all it had taken was a phone call to Sampson to make it happen, no questions asked. Even tonight when Sampson had observed how intently Stern stared through the glass at JoJo, the man hadn't asked any questions. He'd just made his observations—with precision accuracy. Except for the part where Sampson had insinuated that Stern was a man in love.

When Stern walked out on stage he was going to give JoJo the shock of her life. Stern was the last person she expected to see here tonight. And she definitely wouldn't expect him to break up her and Carmichael's little party.

The house lights dimmed for the show and Stern saw Carmichael move from sitting with his back to the stage to sitting beside JoJo to face the stage. It was an understandable move, but it was too close to JoJo for Stern's liking.

He grabbed his violin. He was ready to play and clear

his mind of negative thoughts. Because, right now, quite a few were flowing through his head.

"You know you want to leave here with me, so what are we waiting for?"

JoJo took another sip of her wine and wondered what the jerk sitting beside her was drinking. It had to be something strong if he really believed she wanted to leave here with him. Over the past twenty minutes she had realized just what a mistake she'd made in singling him out as a man worthy of her affection. This man didn't deserve the heart of any woman. The only thing he had on his mind was sex, sex and more sex.

She'd lost count of how many times he'd hinted that he wanted to leave with her. To take her to bed. His, hers, even the nearest hotel would do. Granted she looked different from when he'd seen her last, but now she wondered if she'd had a sign plastered to her forehead during her makeover: Ready to Get Screwed.

Deciding to ignore his last remark, she said, "Oh good, the show is about to begin."

"Come with me and we can have our own show at your place. Or mine."

JoJo drew in a deep breath. She'd encountered very few pushy men in her life, but obnoxious ones she'd come across often enough. Those came into her shop asking specifically for Beeker to work on their cars because she was a female and couldn't possibly know what she was doing. Their way of thinking annoyed her but she'd long ago decided not to lose sleep over it. Men thought what they wanted to think and there was no changing them. Just like Walter. He thought she was easy, but he was wrong. And he thought he was God's gift to women, but he was wrong about that, too. He had spent most of their

conversation bragging. She would never have believed any man could be so into himself.

Walter Carmichael was a real disappointment. After all the work she'd put into transforming herself from a woman no man would look at twice into a woman they looked at…but for all the wrong reasons. Just like Stern had said.

The saddest part was that the person she had hoped Walter would replace in her heart was no longer her best friend. It seemed her obsession with attracting Walter had driven Stern away.

She was glad when the band struck up. Hopefully Walter would shut his mouth and listen for a while. She would stay long enough to enjoy the music, then she would leave and rethink how she could get herself out of the mess she was in with Stern.

After the band had performed a couple of jazzy numbers, an older man, Sampson Kilburn, stepped onstage to a standing ovation. He was the headliner, and she'd heard he was good on the piano. Moments later he proved the rumor true. The man was truly gifted.

"He's good, isn't he?" Walter whispered close to her ear. "As good as I know the two of us will be in bed."

JoJo bit down on her bottom lip, coming close to telling the man to go screw himself. But she didn't bother because at the first intermission she intended to leave.

Stern stood at the glass and stared at JoJo. He wasn't sure what Carmichael had done, but even in the dimly lit room he could tell by her expression that the man had somehow pushed several wrong buttons. That might be good for Stern because he wouldn't have to go through the trouble of breaking up their little party, but it couldn't be good for JoJo.

He knew how much she'd wanted to impress that guy and all the trouble she'd gone through to do so. He hoped she realized the mistakes were not hers; they were all Carmichael's. Now the music he intended to play for her would be more appropriate than ever.

Sweety stuck her head in the door and smiled. "You're up next, Stern. Sampson is bubbling all over himself to have one of his protégés perform with him."

Stern chuckled. "It's really my pleasure. Sampson kept our music lessons real and kept us focused after Mom died. He was even able to handle my baby brother Bane for a while, and that wasn't easy to do."

Moments later, Stern walked with his violin toward where he would stand until he was called out onstage.

Eight

"I'm leaving after this number," JoJo leaned over and whispered to Walter.

"Good. I'll be right behind you."

She frowned. Evidently he had drawn his own conclusions about how this night would end. She figured it was time to let him know, in very clear terms, that when she left she would be leaving alone. However, before she could do so, Sampson Kilburn finished his number and began speaking.

"It gives me great pleasure to bring onstage a former student of mine who I think you're going to enjoy. I want all of you to give a big round of applause for Stern Westmoreland and his violin."

Air left JoJo's lungs as she stared at the stage. *Stern? Here?* She watched as he walked out with his violin, smiling for the audience. She couldn't believe it. What was he doing here? Had he found out this was where she would be? No, how could he have? They hadn't spoken in days. More than likely he had no idea she was in the audience.

She watched as he readied his bow amid whistles and

applause. His smile deepened when he said, "I hope all of you enjoy my musical rendition of this song about true beauty. I'm dedicating this to a special lady in the audience, Jovonnie Jones."

For the second time in less than ten minutes, air left JoJo's lungs. Stern's gaze unerringly found hers and he smiled. He *had* known she was here. But how?

"Hey, that guy's talking about you. You know him?" Walter asked, sounding annoyed.

"Yes, I know him," she said, trying not to show any emotion. "He's my best friend."

"Best friend," he snorted. "Yeah, right. When it comes to a man's and a woman's relationship, there's no such thing."

Whatever words Walter said after that were drowned out when Stern lifted the violin to his shoulder. Accompanied by the band and Sampson at the piano, he played, moving the bow across the strings to produce perfect notes. JoJo had heard that particular song many times, but not until now had she truly been pulled into the melody. Stern was putting his heart and soul into the music and she couldn't help but recall how he'd taught her to play that same instrument when they were in high school.

She felt Walter tug at her hand. "Come on, we were about to leave. If that guy's your best friend, as you claim, then you can hear him play anytime."

JoJo ignored Walter's rudeness as she continued to sit at her table, totally mesmerized by the sight of Stern playing his violin. She was in awe of his skill, as was everyone else in the room.

She'd heard him play a number of times, but tonight was different. He was playing for her. Knowing he'd selected that piece for her sent a warm, fuzzy feeling through her. Somehow, and she wasn't sure how, he'd known she would be here. And somehow he'd also known that tonight hadn't gone as she'd hoped it would. Somehow her best friend had known. And he was here, making her feel beautiful nonetheless.

He continued to play and hold her gaze. In her heart and in her mind she felt he was affirming that no matter what, their friendship could withstand anything. Even the Walter Carmichaels of the world.

At the end, when Stern lowered his violin, he got a standing ovation. On wobbly legs she stood and clapped until her hands began to hurt. He winked at her, and she couldn't help but laugh and wink back. They had a lot to talk about, but she was just happy that her best friend was back.

"Okay, I'm ready to leave," Walter said again. He had stood and was tugging at her arm with a little more force.

She snatched her arm away. "Then by all means go, but I'm not going with you."

Walter's eyes darkened to a cold stony black. "Moments before your *best friend* took to the stage, you suggested we leave."

JoJo frowned as she sat back down. "I suggested no such thing. I told you I was leaving. At no time did I invite you to leave with me."

He leaned down near her face. "Don't you dare tease me. I don't take kindly to women who play with me. I don't think you know who you're messing with."

"And I don't think you know who you're messing with."

JoJo blinked when Walter's face broke into a smile. "Okay, I get it. You like being the dominant one. This time I'll let you, but when we get to your place we'll reverse roles."

JoJo tilted her head and stared at him. Was he crazy?

She stood up and parted her lips to give him the put-down of his life when Stern approached.

"Is everything all right?" he asked.

She saw the concern in his gaze. "Yes, everything is all right. I've got this."

"Okay."

She knew Stern agreed to stay out of it only because he knew she had it under control. Turning to Walter, she said, "Read my lips, Walter. I am not going anywhere with you and you aren't going anywhere with me. I misjudged your character and evidently you've misjudged mine. Now get out of my face."

The stony look returned to Walter's gaze. "I don't like being made a fool of. I am not wrong about you. You walked into this club dressed like a woman anxious to get laid."

JoJo quickly reached out and touched Stern's hand when he took a step toward Walter. "No, Stern," she said firmly. Her eyes flashed fire as she stared at Walter, fully aware that people were beginning to stare. "I don't like a man assuming things about me and treating me with disrespect."

"Respect? I can treat you anyway I please," he said with a sneer. "Do you know who I am?"

JoJo narrowed her gaze. "Yes, a little boy in a man's suit who needs to grow up."

A few chuckles came from behind them, from the bar where his friends were still standing. Walter Carmichael had the good sense not to say anything else. Instead he gave JoJo another glacier-cold look before walking out of the club.

"You okay, JoJo?"

She slid her gaze from the club's exit door to Stern. "Why wouldn't I be?"

Stern touched one of the curls in her hair before running a slow hand down the side of her face and touching the collar of her dress. "Because you did all of this for him," he whispered. "I'm sorry."

She drew in a deep breath, tempted to say that she'd only done it for Walter as a way to forget about Stern. The last thing she wanted was for Stern to feel sorry for her, especially when she was trying hard not to feel sorry for herself.

"It's okay. I'm fine. Thanks for the musical piece you performed. It was beautiful and touching. I felt special. How did you know I was here?"

Stern looked around and she noticed at the same time he did that they still had an audience. "I don't have another performance tonight," he said. "Come on, I'll follow you home and then we can talk."

She nodded and together they walked out of the club.

"I'm making coffee. You want a cup?"

Kicking off her shoes, JoJo entered her living room and watched Stern head for her kitchen. "Yes," she called out after him. "And you know how I like it."

She placed her purse on the table and eased down onto the sofa, thinking about how badly things had gone tonight. Perhaps she should have done something differently? She hadn't teased Walter as he'd claimed. They had been having a conversation about a recent movie when suddenly, without warning, he shifted the conversation to sex. Rather explicit sex. He told her right out what he liked women to do for him and that he thought a roll between the sheets was a great way for two people to get to know each other. Then he tried to talk her into leaving with him.

"Don't do that," Stern said, coming back into the room and taking the wingback chair across from her.

"What?"

"Gnaw off your bottom lip. He's not worth it."

"I know but..."

"But what?"

"But I can't help wondering what makes some men turn into total jerks."

Stern leaned forward and stared at her for a moment. "What exactly did he do to get you so riled?"

"He insisted that I sleep with him. Tonight. Dammit, Stern, we hadn't even kissed yet. All he wanted, all he was looking for, was a one-night stand. I wanted more. I wanted to develop a relationship with him. I thought he would be someone I truly wanted to get to know better."

"He didn't deserve the things you wanted, JoJo."

"I know." She rested her head against the sofa cushion to stare up at the ceiling. "So you want to tell me how you happened to be there tonight?"

He stood. "Let me pour our coffee and then we'll talk."

JoJo lowered her head and watched him leave the room. It was so unfair that the guy she'd fallen in love with was the one person she could not have. She heard Stern in her kitchen, opening cabinets to get two coffee cups. He knew his way around her house as much as she knew her way around his, and he didn't hesitate making himself at home whenever he visited. It was the same with her whenever she was over at his place. No limitations and no restrictions. As far as she knew, she was the only nonfamily member who had a key to his place.

He came back into the room carrying a tray with two cups and her coffeepot. He proceeded to pour the hot liquid into their cups. "I thought about making you tea instead. Drinking this will probably keep you up tonight."

She had news for him. She would probably be up late tonight anyway, trying to recover from everything that had happened. She took the cup from him. "Thanks." She took a sip knowing she would enjoy it. Stern had a knack for making good coffee.

She watched as he returned to the chair he had been sitting in earlier. Why did they have to be best friends? If they weren't best friends, then...

She drew in a deep breath and stared down into her cup.

If he wasn't your best friend, then he would have no reason to be sitting in your living room, tonight or any night. He probably wouldn't even know you existed. Men who look like Stern don't date girls who do what you do for a living. And when they do, they are only after one thing.

She frowned, refusing to lump Stern into the same category as Walter.

"You're frowning, JoJo. Is the coffee that bad?"

She shook her head and looked over at him. "No, I was just thinking."

"About Walter?"

No, you. Instead she said, "Yes, Walter." That was partly true.

He took a sip of his own coffee. "May I ask you something?"

"Yes?" she replied.

"What did you ever see in him?"

JoJo couldn't help but chuckle. Only a man would ask a question like that. Although Walter had acted like a total jerk tonight, that did not change the fact that he was a nice-looking man. "Um, possibilities."

She figured they should leave it at that for now, especially because she had her own questions. "You knew I would be at the Punch Bowl tonight. How?"

He stretched his long legs out in front of him and leaned back in her chair. "I have my sources. Since you refused to tell me where you were going or the name of the man you were interested in, I decided to do my own investigation."

She nodded. It wouldn't be hard to find out his source because she knew every single person who had the information. She met his gaze. "You didn't return my calls."

She watched as he looked down into his coffee cup, seeming to gather his thoughts. He then looked back at her. "No, I didn't. I needed time to think."

"About that kiss we shared?" There was no reason not to directly address what she knew had bothered him.

"Yes, about that kiss we shared."

"But why? We knew starting out that the kiss meant nothing, Stern. We even talked about it before we did it. I don't understand why you made such a big deal out of it when you were merely helping me improve my skills."

Stern looked down into his cup of coffee again. How could he explain to JoJo that the kiss did mean something? Although he'd wanted to believe that kiss had been about helping her improve her skills, in fact it had not been about that at all, which was why he'd felt the need to back off. Now he wondered if what Zane had said, and what Sampson had alluded to, were true. Was Stern beginning to feel something for JoJo that had nothing to do with friendship but everything to do with a man desiring a woman?

Even now, she was sitting across from him looking sexier than he'd ever seen her look. He could see why all the men at the bar had been so taken with her tonight.

Whoever had performed her makeover had done an outstanding job.

But then, that was part of the problem. The makeover only emphasized the beauty on the outside. Those other men had failed to see the beauty that was on the inside. In his opinion, she hadn't needed a makeover to emphasize that beauty. It was always there with her. Carmichael hadn't wanted to see past her looks.

"Stern?"

He drew in a deep breath and decided to answer her question truthfully…as best he could. "Yes, we talked about the kiss and it was supposed to be nothing more than a way to improve your skills. However, I lost control, JoJo, and I shouldn't have. If your phone hadn't interrupted us, I would have tried stripping you naked."

She held his gaze for a moment before waving off his words. "You would have stopped."

"No, I wouldn't have. Hell, JoJo, I had unbuttoned your blouse."

And she had let him, which proved just how much she had trusted him to do the right thing. But, at the time, doing the right thing had been the last thought on his mind.

"So you unbuttoned my blouse—no big deal."

He wondered why she was making light of what he'd done when he had taken his inappropriate behavior seriously. He hadn't been able to sleep much that night, but it hadn't been remorse that had kept him awake. It had been the memory of how aroused he'd gotten from touching her skin and kissing her lips. Why, after all these years, was he being drawn to her this way? Why, all of a sudden, was there this full-blown attraction he couldn't fight?

"Although Walter was a big disappointment," JoJo said, interrupting his thoughts, "I don't think this weekend was a complete waste. I got to spend time with your cousins and sisters-in-law. Ritz and his assistant were a hoot and I liked the way they did my hair and makeup. They even told me how to apply the makeup myself if I ever decide to indulge again. So I should thank you for suggesting the makeover. "

He wasn't sure she should thank him. He wasn't all that concerned about things not working out with Carmichael because he had planned to sabotage that anyway. He might as well come clean about that, too.

"I have a confession to make."

She glanced over at him. "What?"

"I didn't want you and Carmichael to hook up tonight. In fact, I was hoping you wouldn't. I had even planned to do something to interrupt you if the two of you left together."

JoJo lifted a brow. "Do what?"

"Become a nuisance. And when Sampson told me what a jerk Carmichael can be with women—to the point that he's rumored to have roughed up a few who dismissed his advances—I knew I didn't want you with him."

She got up from the sofa and moved to where he'd placed the tray with the coffeepot. She poured another cup. His gaze followed her movements in that too-sexy dress. She'd removed those killer stilettos and was in her bare feet, allowing him to appreciate her gorgeous legs.

"Want some more?" she asked, turning around.

He met her eyes. "What?"

"Coffee."

"No, I'm good," he said, taking a sip and wishing he had something stronger. His attraction to her tonight was fiercer than ever. That's the last thing either of them needed. She needed a shoulder to cry on, not a friend with a hard-on. And he felt himself getting harder as he watched her walk back over to the sofa and tuck her legs beneath her, which raised the hem of her dress and gave him a glimpse of luscious thighs. He knew it was time for him to go, but there was no way he could stand up just yet.

She took a slow sip of her coffee before meeting his gaze. "Explain something to me, Stern."

"I will if I can."

"You didn't know Walter. Why wouldn't you want things to have worked out for us?"

"I told you what Sampson said."

She nodded. "So, you only planned to make a nuisance of yourself after finding out about Walter's character?"

"No."

He saw her forehead crease and figured he was confusing her. There had always been total honesty between him and JoJo, which was why their friendship had lasted so long and had remained so strong.

"Let me explain something to you about men in general, JoJo. We're made to desire women and made to want to make love to women."

She frowned. "Please tell me you're not trying to justify Walter's behavior."

Stern shook his head. "No, definitely not. Mainly because a real man also knows how to respect a woman. Not to talk down to her. You were right on point when you said he was acting like a little boy in a suit, although I don't think he liked hearing it."

"I was just being honest."

"Well, there are some who don't prefer honesty."

She shrugged. "Then it's their problem, not mine." She took another sip of her coffee.

Stern watched her. What was it about being here with her, alone, tonight? He'd done exactly this a number of other times without feeling anything more than friendship. It could be the way she looked tonight, sexy, displaying all those attributes she usually kept well hidden.

She looked good in that dress, with red on her sultry lips and those sexy earrings dangling from her ears. And damn, what was that fragrance she was wearing? It was such an alluring scent. Her hair, styled in feathery layers around her face, brought out the darkness of her eyes, the fullness of her cheekbones and the lushness of her mouth. He was tempted to move close to her and run his fingers through the silken strands of her hair right before taking her sultry lips with his. Were things just as Zane claimed? Had Stern's feelings for JoJo shifted without him realizing it?

"So why did you plan to make a nuisance of yourself, Stern? Especially when you knew all the trouble I'd gone through to make a good impression on Walter?"

Something inside of him almost snapped. Why was she so fixated on Walter Carmichael? He mentally replayed everything that had happened between them since that day at the lodge when she'd asked him how to make a man want her. His jealousy for the unknown man had started then and it had increased each and every time she'd brought up this mystery man.

"Stern?"

He gave her a sharp look. "Do you really want to know?"

"Of course I want to know," she said in exasperation.

He'd tried to explain it before but for some reason she just wasn't getting it. "What if I said I didn't like the idea of you chasing behind a man?"

She lifted her chin. "I wasn't chasing behind him, not exactly. I saw him and decided he had potential. He would do."

He lifted a brow. "Do for what?"

"Doesn't matter."

He thought it did. As far as he knew, JoJo had never been intimate with a guy. Had she selected Carmichael as the man she'd wanted to share her first sexual encounter with? JoJo would not sleep with someone she didn't care about, so Carmichael had blown his chance when he'd tried making her a one-night stand.

Stern stood. "Whatever the reason, it did matter." He placed his cup down on the tray. "Come on and walk me to the door. It's getting late."

He went over to her and reached out his hand. She took it as she stood. He couldn't resist letting his gaze move up and down her body. "You look beautiful tonight, JoJo."

She smiled as she walked him to the door. "I actually felt beautiful tonight. I'll do this again. The hair, the makeup, the dress. It's a good change."

"Yes," he said when they came to a stop in front of the door. "It's a nice change."

Giving in to temptation, he locked a curl of her hair around his finger. "You didn't cut it."

"No, I didn't cut it. Ritz just trimmed the ends."

"Whatever he did, I like it."

"Thanks."

"Don't cover it up with a cap for a while."

She chuckled. "Can't make you that promise. Can you see me changing spark plugs with curls falling in my face?"

He grinned then. "I guess not."

"But Ritz showed me how to work it back into this style whenever I want to."

Stern didn't know what there was about her hair that made him want to go after her lips whenever he put his hands in it. He felt himself staring deeply into her eyes. Then, as if of its own accord, his mouth slowly inched closer to hers. Why was his body aching so intensely to hold her in his arms?

The moment their lips touched, merged, latched together in a hungry connection, she let out a small gasp. Whether it was one of shock or one of pleasure, he wasn't sure. All he knew was that she tasted of sweet coffee and he wanted to consume every inch of her mouth.

The moment she leaned into him, his hands automatically left her head to wrap around her waist as their tongues dueled in a fiery exchange. There had been no reason to kiss her tonight. But then he quickly decided that yes, there had been. Tonight she was a woman who deserved a man's attention and he had no problem giving it to her.

He finally released her mouth, then leaned in and kissed around her lips several more times, inhaling her scent and feeling her quiver in his arms. And just like with those other kisses, she had again followed his lead. She'd kissed him back just now in a way that made him want to kiss her that much more.

"Stern?"

"Hmm?" he said as he continued to place soft kisses around her mouth.

"Why are you kissing me?"

"Because I want to."

He hadn't said it to be smart. He was being completely honest with her. So he decided to carry that honesty a little further. He pulled back slightly and touched her chin with the tip of his finger, tilting it up to give her another full kiss on the lips. "In case you haven't figured it out yet, JoJo, there's something happening between us that I don't think either of us expected."

"What?"

He smiled as he took a step backward. Instead of answering her question, he said, "I'm leaving town on Monday for a business trip to Florida and won't be back until Thursday. Let's do something when I get back."

"All right. What about going bowling on Friday night?"

"How about the lodge?"

She raised a brow. "The lodge?"

"Yes. Let's spend the weekend at the lodge."

"But we just got back from the lodge."

"And I want to go again," he said. "Something is happening between us. I don't know what it is, JoJo, but I think maybe it's time we find out."

He leaned in and kissed her lips again before opening the door to leave.

Nine

"Hey, JoJo, you need to look like a girl more often," Sony Wyatt said, grinning. He was standing with a group of guys who worked at the shop as they passed around her pictures from Saturday night. She had brought them in for Beeker and Wanda, but it seemed the pictures were now making the rounds.

"Funny, Sony," she said, grabbing a hose to flush out the carburetor of the car she was working on and ignoring the men's whistles as they looked through the pictures.

"You don't look like the same person," Leon Shaw, another worker, added.

She rolled her eyes. "Well, I am the same person, and need I remind the four of you that I am also your boss? So be nice."

"Did Stern see these?" Charlie Dixon wanted to know.

She lifted her head from underneath the hood of the car. All the guys who worked for her knew that she and Stern were best friends. "Why?"

"Just wondering."

She shrugged and placed her head back under the hood

to finish up the work on the Corvette. Charlie would be surprised to know Stern hadn't needed to see the pictures because he had seen the real thing. In fact, she was still trying to wrap her mind around just what had happened Saturday night from the time she'd walked into the Punch Bowl and met Walter's gaze to later that same night when Stern had kissed her good-night in her foyer. Even now, she was tempted to touch her lips to remember what she'd felt at the kiss he had placed there.

And it had been a real kiss. Nothing he'd done as part of any lesson. She had enjoyed it, and she had a feeling he had, too. For a moment, they had forgotten they were nothing but best friends and had kissed like…like two people attracted to each other. Even now she couldn't understand it. Oh, she understood perfectly from her end because she was in love with him. But what had driven him to kiss her like that? That's what confused her more than anything, and she wouldn't be satisfied until she found out the answer.

At least he was aware something was going on. Before he'd left his exact words had been, *"In case you haven't figured it out yet, JoJo, there's something happening between us that I don't think either of us expected."*

She drew in a deep breath, wondering if there was a way she could multiply those feelings so he'd realize the full extent of what was happening. It had already happened to her. How could she make sure it happened to him?

A few hours later, back in her office doing paperwork and still trying to wrap her mind around everything about this past Saturday night, Wanda knocked on the door. Recognizing the knock, JoJo called out for her to come in.

"Apparently you didn't tell me everything about Saturday night," Wanda said, entering the office and taking the chair across from JoJo's desk.

Knowing she wouldn't be getting any work done for the next minute or so, JoJo closed the file she was working on. "And just what do you think I didn't tell you?"

"How you apparently pissed off Walter Carmichael."

JoJo nibbled her bottom lip. She'd told Wanda the same thing she'd told anyone else who'd asked about Saturday night: things between her and Walter hadn't worked out and when they left the club they'd gone their separate ways. That hadn't been a lie...she'd just deliberately left out everything involving Stern. "What makes you think I pissed him off?" she asked, even though she knew she had.

"Because he just called Beeker and wants his auto records transferred to Carl's Automotive across town. He told Beeker he doesn't plan on ever coming back here again."

JoJo stood and crossed the room to pull open a drawer in the file cabinet. "Great! He's the last person I want to see anyway," she said, pulling out Walter's folder and slamming the drawer shut. She then went back to her desk, sat down and handed the folder to Wanda.

Wanda leaned back in her chair. "Hmm, so tell me, JoJo. How can there be trouble in paradise when you hadn't quite reached the island yet?"

JoJo looked across her desk at Wanda. "Do you really want to know?" Before Wanda could respond, she said, "Then I'll tell you." She allowed herself an irritated breath before saying, "Walter Carmichael is a jerk who assumed I had gotten all dolled up on Saturday night just so he could poke me. All he did the entire evening was try to talk me into leaving the club with him so we could find the nearest bed. What ever happened to two people getting to know each other first?"

Wanda smiled. "I think that went out the window when women became just as interested in one-night stands as men. Couples don't want to get to know each other anymore. All they want is to get into each other."

"Well, that's not what I want."

Wanda nodded. "And I assume you told him that and he didn't take it well."

JoJo rolled her eyes. "Like I said, the man's a jerk. How could I ever have thought he and I could get something going?"

"So, your plan to replace Stern in your heart didn't work. What do you plan to do now?" Wanda asked.

JoJo closed the file on her desk again and leaned back in her chair. "Nothing. I'll grow old and die a virgin."

"Doesn't have to be that way, you know."

JoJo bristled at Wanda's words. "It does have to be that way. At least for me it does. I'm not into one-night stands or casual sex, and there hasn't been another guy who has caught my eye."

"Then don't concentrate on another guy. Just concentrate on the guy you really want."

"Oh, please, I wish it was that simple. But as you know Stern is off-limits."

"Why? Because he's your best friend?"

"Yes."

Wanda didn't say anything for a moment. "Haven't you ever heard of friends with benefits?"

"Of course."

"Then get with the program."

JoJo shook her head. Wanda was old enough to be her mother and the woman was promoting sex. "That sort of thing wouldn't work for me and Stern, either. We aren't

just friends—we're *best* friends. Besides, he's still freak-
ing out over those kisses."

Too late she realized what she'd said and quickly
opened the folder again when Wanda sat up straight in
her chair and stared at her. JoJo knew the possibility
that the woman hadn't caught her last sentence was too
much to hope for.

"What kisses? You and Stern *kissed?*" Wanda ex-
claimed after sucking in a shocked breath. "And don't
you dare shut up on me now, JoJo. You might as well tell
all. Don't let me ask Stern for the—"

"You wouldn't dare," JoJo said, rising from her seat
to lean over her desk toward Wanda.

Wanda's blue eyes shot up as she leaned forward, too.
"Wanna bet?"

No, JoJo didn't want to bet. She had all but admitted to Wanda last week that she had fallen in love with
Stern and she wouldn't put it past Wanda to try her hand
at matchmaking. "Okay, we kissed. More than once."

"And?"

JoJo rolled her eyes. Did the woman need all the details? "I enjoyed it and I believe he did, too. It started
out as a lesson on how to improve my kissing technique
for Walter and—"

"You've got to be kidding," Wanda interrupted in an
incredulous tone.

"No, I'm not kidding."

"And Stern went along with it? Giving you kissing
lessons for Walter?"

"Yes, and then he felt bad because he lost control."

JoJo wondered at the smile that touched Wanda's lips.
"Go ahead, JoJo. I'm still listening."

"Well, anyway, we kissed again Saturday night after
he took me home."

Wanda raised a brow. "Saturday night? After he took you home?"

"Yes." Seeing no way out of it, JoJo leaned back in her chair and decided to tell Wanda the whole story.

"Wow," Wanda said, after JoJo finished telling her what happened. "So you and Stern are going to the lodge this weekend to figure out things."

JoJo shrugged. "He's the one who has to figure things out. I already know why I get into our kisses. But I'm sure it has to be confusing for him since he doesn't feel about me the way I feel about him."

"Are you sure that he doesn't?"

"Of course, I'm sure. Why would he?"

Now it was Wanda's turn to shrug. "Um, I don't know. It could be because you're a nice person, the two of you have a special relationship and he knows you better than anyone. It could also be that he sees what others don't see."

"What?"

"The fact that you have inner beauty *and* outer beauty."

JoJo shook her head. "Thanks, but no. With Stern, it's a man's thing. He all but said so Saturday night. That's why he lost control."

"But he knows something is happening between the two of you and he's willing to investigate to find out what, right?"

"Yes."

A huge smile spread across Wanda's face. "Then use this weekend to your advantage. You already love him, so do whatever it takes to make him fall in love with you."

JoJo frowned. "I may not know a lot about men, but what I do know is that a woman can't make a man fall in love with her."

"There is a possibility she can. Especially if he's half-way there. So take a chance and shock Stern this weekend. Suggest that the two of you become best friends with benefits and see what happens."

"So, how was the trip?" Riley asked, entering his brother's office.

"Great," Stern said, smiling as he looked up from a stack of papers. "That land deal in Florida is a go."

Riley smiled. "Good news to hear. And I also hear you're headed back to the lodge this weekend."

"Yes, both JoJo and I need a break."

"The two of you just got back less than two weeks ago," Riley said, sliding into the chair across from Stern's desk.

"And we're going again. We enjoy it there."

"Apparently. And I saw the pictures that Megan took of JoJo's makeover. She looked gorgeous. I'd forgotten how much hair she had under those caps she likes wearing. And those legs. Wow!"

Stern frowned. "Aren't you getting married at the end of this month?"

Riley threw his head back and laughed. "Yes, but I can still appreciate a beautiful woman when I see one. And don't worry. Alpha has my heart, totally and completely. Who has yours?"

Stern lifted a brow. "My what?"

"Your heart."

A sly grin touched Stern's lips. "Okay, I admit it. Alpha has my heart totally and completely, as well."

"Smart-ass," Riley said, chuckling. "You know what I'm asking."

"No," Stern said, shaking his head. "Honestly, I don't."

"If you don't, I have a feeling it won't be long now

before you do," Riley said, standing and heading for the door.

"What do you mean by that?" Stern called out.

Riley paused before he opened the door and glanced back at Stern. "Man, you're in love and don't even know it."

A short while later Stern stood in his office, looking out the window. Now yet another person assumed more was going on between him and JoJo than just friendship. In a way, he shouldn't be surprised by Riley's assumption. Zane claimed most of the family believed there was more going on.

Riley was wrong. He *already* knew how he felt about JoJo. He had fought the truth for as long as he could but would now admit that he'd fallen in love with her. He might have loved her all along like Zane and the others suspected, or he might have realized his true feelings just recently. It didn't matter at this point. The most important thing was that he loved her.

But that only compounded his problems.

He wasn't a man who pined after a woman, but he had longed for JoJo this week. He had talked to her every night on the phone while in Florida but it seemed as if she deliberately kept the conversations brief. He wasn't sure if he'd imagined it or not. But, to be fair to her, she'd had busy days this week and had wanted to get to bed early. It wasn't her fault that he had missed her, ached for her, yearned for her.

He had found himself watching the clock and counting the days. Thursday hadn't gotten here soon enough to suit him. He had planned to stop by the shop after he'd landed and left the airport. But when he called, Wanda told him JoJo had left early for a dentist's appointment.

So, instead of going straight home he had come into the office instead.

Now he couldn't wait until tomorrow. Until this weekend.

Because he realized that Zane was right and Stern wanted more than just friendship with JoJo. He wanted forever. But how was he supposed to change the nature of their relationship without scaring her off?

Zane had made another prediction, too, one Stern hadn't bought into. For some reason, Zane suspected JoJo might have feelings for him. Stern would admit he had racked his brain trying to recall a time recently when those feelings had been displayed and he couldn't think of one. For the past few weeks she had been into Walter Carmichael and trying to turn herself into the object of the man's affections. Well, Carmichael had blown it and lost out. As far as Stern was concerned it was his turn to do something the other man hadn't done: win JoJo's heart.

Stern shoved his hands into his pants pockets. Tomorrow evening he and JoJo would leave town for the six-hour drive to his hunting lodge for the weekend. During that time he would make his move. They'd be returning on Sunday, so he would only have Saturday night.

He had one night. One night to prove that they could move their relationship to a whole new level and become much more than best friends.

Ten

Stern tilted his Stetson back and blinked several times when JoJo opened her door. "Your hair."

"What about it?" she asked, handing him her overnight bag.

"It looks like it did Saturday night."

JoJo chuckled as she pulled the door shut and locked it behind her. "Is that a crime?"

"No, but I didn't expect it."

There will be a lot happening this weekend that you won't expect, she thought as they walked to his four-wheel-drive SUV. "I told you that Ritz showed me how to do it myself when I'm not wearing my cap. Of course it doesn't look as good as when he did it, but it will suffice."

"Well, I think you did a great job."

"Thanks. How was your trip?"

"It was okay. I missed you, though," he said, putting her bag next to his in the backseat.

JoJo couldn't ignore the flutters in her stomach as he opened the car door for her. This was not the first time he'd gone away on a trip and come back to tell her he'd missed her. But this time felt different. Of course, it was all in her mind, but still.

"I missed you, too," she said, meaning it. Although they had talked every night, she had deliberately kept the calls short, afraid she would slip and say something stupid—like confessing she loved him.

"Anything interesting happen at work this week?" he asked after getting in the car and snapping on his seat belt. It was then that he turned those dark, sexy eyes on her.

She sucked in a breath. It was as if she'd taken a dose of some kind of sexual stimulant. The air suddenly felt charged. She could place the blame on all those dreams she'd had about him all week. Or that romance novel she'd read this week thanks to Wanda. The love scenes had almost blistered her fingers they'd been so hot.

"Nothing happened. Except Walter called Beeker on Monday and transferred his auto records. I guess I've lost him as a customer."

"You don't sound too sad about it."

She smiled. "I'm not. So how did things go with you in Florida? Did you close the deal?"

"Yes."

Her smile widened. "I'm happy for you."

"Thanks."

She reclined her seat. Stern preferred to do all the driving. All she had to do was sit back and relax or take a nap.

"Tired?" he asked when he came to a traffic light.

"Yes. Busy week. Any weekends when I can get away are nice. Thanks for inviting me to come with you."

"You're always welcome."

She wondered if she would be welcome when she brought up the next topic of conversation. Even though Wanda had been the one to suggest it, the more JoJo thought about it, the more she liked the idea of them becoming best friends with benefits. She just wasn't sure how receptive Stern would be to the idea.

She glanced over at him. "Stern?"

"Hmm?"

"I've been thinking."

"What about?"

"You. Me. Our relationship."

He quickly glanced over at her before returning his eyes to the road. "What about our relationship?"

"We've been best friends forever."

"True."

"And there's no other man I trust more."

"Thanks."

"I'm getting older."

"So am I," he countered.

She nodded and smiled. "Okay, we're both getting older, but there are plenty of things you've done that I haven't tried yet."

"Such as?"

"Sex."

Stern braked to avoid running into the back of the car in front of him. He then checked his rearview mirror before pulling to the side of the road. Killing the engine, he turned to JoJo. "What did you say?"

JoJo didn't realize she'd been holding her breath until now. She began nibbling on her bottom lip while he stared at her. "I said, you've had sex and I haven't."

"Were we supposed to be competing or something?" he asked, frowning.

She could feel heat gathering in her cheeks. Of all the topics they'd talked about over the years, sex had never been one of them. She'd only known that he'd become sexually active when she found condom packs in his belongings. Once, a pack had fallen out of his book bag at school, and she had quickly picked them up and given them back to him. All that day she'd wondered if what she'd heard about him and Melanie Hargrove was true.

"Nah, we weren't competing, Stern. I was just making an observation."

"Why?"

"Why?" she repeated.

"Yes, why?"

She nibbled on her bottom lip again. "I'm in a dilemma."

He frowned. "What kind of dilemma?"

"I'll be thirty in a few months."

"And?"

"And I'm still a virgin."

She watched the way his Adam's apple moved in his throat. "So?"

She shrugged. "So, I know it's my problem, but I was hoping you could help me out."

"How?"

His curt questions were beginning to annoy her. "How?" she repeated.

"Yes, how? How can I help you out?" he asked.

"By agreeing to do something."

He raised a brow. "What?"

She drew in a deep breath. "By agreeing that we become best friends with benefits."

Stern could only stare at her. Of all the things he'd assumed she would ask, *that* was not it. Never in a thousand years would he have expected a request like that to flow from her lips. But she had asked, and whether she knew it or not—and he was certain that she probably didn't—she had made things easy for him. All last night and earlier today he had racked his brain trying to figure out how he would seduce her without coming across as a jerk like Walter Carmichael.

At one point, he'd decided that just coming out and confessing that he loved her would be the best thing to do. But then he doubted that she was truly ready to believe him. So he'd decided that his original plan—to use their one night to prove that they could be more than best friends—was the best way to go.

Now, though, she had taken the decision out of his hands and he planned to run with it. All he had to do was go along with her idea and he'd have his chance to prove to her that best friends with benefits could easily transform their relationship into something more meaningful and everlasting.

And there was no doubt in his mind he wanted forever with JoJo.

"Okay," he said.

"Okay?" she asked, staring at him.

"Yes, okay. Best friends with benefits it is."

She lifted her brow. "You're agreeing? Just like that?"

"Yes. Were you expecting me not to?"

She shrugged. "I guess not. But I *had* expected you to think about it."

"What's there to think about? I want you."

She looked surprised. "You do?"

"Yes. I had time to think about us when I was in Florida, and I believe one of the reasons I have a tendency to lose control when we kiss is because deep down I want you. That explains a lot of things."

"It does?"

"Yes. I guess the desire has been there for a while and kissing you brought it to the forefront."

"Oh."

"But then I need to be sure that you want me and that I'm not a replacement for Walter Carmichael."

"You're not."

He thought she sounded pretty sure of it. "Are you certain?"

"I'm positive. I didn't know Walter, but I thought I wanted to get to know him. In the end, I discovered he wasn't anyone I wanted to know after all."

"So you hadn't fallen in love with him?"

"Of course not! In fact, I can't believe he's the one I picked to replace—"

She stopped talking rather abruptly, leading him to believe she'd almost said something she hadn't wanted to say.

"He's the one you picked to replace what?" he inquired.

"Nothing. Not important."

He remembered having bits and pieces of this same conversation before and suspected she was hiding something that *was* important. "Okay, so we're in agreement that our relationship will be changing. Right?"

"Right."

He smiled as he pressed the keyless ignition back on. "You sound tired. Why don't you relax and take a nap. I'll wake you when we get to the lodge."

"All right."

Stern watched as she closed her eyes. She looked beautiful while asleep. When he'd picked her up and she'd opened her front door he had blinked when he saw her hairstyle. And instead of wearing jeans she had on a denim skirt with leggings and boots. Her attire was definitely new and she looked damn cute. But she still looked like JoJo. *His* JoJo.

As he headed the car toward the interstate, the knowledge that she didn't do casual sex weighed heavily on his mind. So if she was willing to experiment with him in the bedroom, that meant something. Hell, he hoped it did.

Could Zane have been right on all accounts? Could JoJo feel something more than friendship for him, too? But if that was the case, why had she gone after Walter Carmichael? Stern wasn't sure, but he was determined to find out.

"It won't take but a minute to start up the fireplace, JoJo."

"Okay."

JoJo looked around. She loved it here and always enjoyed coming to the lodge with Stern. It seemed fitting that any change in their relationship should take place here, where she had first realized she loved him. Shivers raced through her at the thought that they would probably share a bed tonight. She'd dreamed of him for months and months. At some point while she was here all of her dreams would come true.

She jumped when Stern eased up behind her and placed his jacket around her shoulders. She glanced up at him. "What's this for?"

"You were quivering. For you, that means you're cold or nervous. If it's the latter, you have no reason to be nervous with me, JoJo. No matter what might change, I won't. I'll still be your Stern."

Her Stern... Boy, she wished. She knew in the real world, a lot of women would love to make that claim. He'd always been a heartthrob and she had found the number of women who had envied their relationship amusing. She was certain there were some women who still did envy them. She knew there were some who ques-

tioned their relationship, too. But never had Stern let any
of them diminish their friendship. She'd heard he'd put
several women in their place when they had tried.

She watched him walk back over to the fireplace. Usually, he would call ahead to have Mr. Richardson, the
older man he paid to look out for the lodge, get the fireplace roaring with heat before they arrived.

"Did you forget to call Mr. Richardson?" she asked.

He was kneeling and she couldn't help but appreciate
the way his jeans stretched tight over his muscular thighs.
And that blue sweater he was wearing looked good on
him. She'd known it would when she'd purchased it for
him last year as a Christmas present. He had just the
chest for it, hard-muscled and solid.

While she was thinking of all the things she'd done
to that chest in her dreams, he glanced over his shoulder
at her and said, "No, I didn't forget. He and Mrs. Richardson left a couple of days ago for a two-week cruise to
Hawaii. It's their fiftieth wedding anniversary."

She smiled. "That's wonderful. We need to send them
a gift when we get back."

He returned her smile. "Yes, we do." He then went
back to starting the fire.

She could stand there and ogle him all night but decided she needed to help in some way, to stay busy for
a while. It was way past midnight, but because she had
slept on the long drive here, she was wide-awake. "I'll go
upstairs and check the bedrooms...I mean the *bedroom*...
to make sure it's okay." Oops. Already she'd forgotten
they would need only one bedroom because they would
be sharing a bed.

He straightened to stand. "Come here for a minute,
JoJo."

Swallowing deeply, she crossed the room and came to a stop in front of him. "Yes?"

She couldn't help noticing that he was staring at her mouth. And then instead of answering her, he leaned down and captured her lips with his. She heard herself moan on a breathless sigh, which gave him the opening he needed. Immediately, his tongue slid between her lips and lured her into a mating that made her wrap her arms around his neck.

Stern knew how to do more than stoke the fire in the fireplace because his kiss was definitely stoking the fire in her. His tongue left its mark on every area it touched. Instinctively, she leaned into him and moaned again when she felt his erection pressing into her stomach.

A rush of desire consumed her. She tried calming her body down but couldn't do so. It was as if her mouth had finally gotten what it had longed for. She was consumed with love for him and he was doing a good job stoking their passion. It would not have bothered her in the least if he'd stripped her naked and made love to her right here in front of the fireplace.

Too soon to suit her, he ended the kiss and stepped back, taking her hand in his. "We need to talk, JoJo. While you were asleep in the car, I had six hours to really think about this."

Her heart took a dive into her stomach. "And you've changed your mind about everything." She stated this as if it was a fact and not a question.

Stern wrapped his arms around her waist. "No, I haven't changed my mind. But what I want you to do is really think about what you want for us."

"I know what I want."

"Do you?"

"Yes."

"Are you sure?"

"Yes."

He stared at her for a moment before easing her down with him onto the huge throw rug so they could sit facing the fireplace. "This best friends with benefits thing... What exactly is your definition of it?"

She nibbled at her bottom lip and then said, "Just like it says. Basically we have to be best friends, and we get the benefits of that friendship...which I guess is something we've been doing all along." She paused a moment and said, "Except..."

"Except what?"

"We also get to explore a level of intimacy we haven't explored before."

"You haven't ever slept with a man, JoJo."

"Yes, and that's one of the advantages of friends with benefits. The sex."

"And you only want to indulge in sex because of this age thing?"

"No. I want the sex because I want to know the pleasure I can feel. But I don't want to share it with just anyone, Stern. That would make it too casual for me. Meaningless. Sharing it with you makes it personal. Special. I trust you. And if you're worried that I'd assume there will be a commitment between us, don't be. I know that won't be the case. It will be whatever it is."

He didn't say anything for a minute but looked at her in a way that had her heart jumping. He took a step closer. "Now that's where you're wrong, JoJo. If we start this, it won't be reserved just for when we get an itch to make love. I couldn't handle a relationship with you that way. Somehow it cheapens what we share."

"Oh."

"I couldn't sleep with you tonight and then sleep with

someone else next week. That would make me no better than the Walter Carmichaels of the world. If we become best friends with benefits, we'll also become a couple."

"We will?"

"Yes."

"And you'd want that?"

"Why wouldn't I want it?"

She shrugged. "Your lifestyle. You're single and you've stayed that way for a reason."

"Yes, but then so have you, right?"

"Yes, but it's different for me. There's not a flock of men running behind me like the flock of women running behind you. You seem to like the chase and I can't see you giving it up."

"I will give it up. I'll be dating you. Only you."

She frowned. "But will I be enough?"

He smiled. "Oh, yes, you'll be enough."

She was skeptical. "This is going to be harder than I thought."

"Why?"

"I honestly never thought of us dating exclusively," she said.

"But you have thought of us having sex?"

She figured she could be honest with him about that. She didn't want him to think that her desire to be intimate with him was just a hormonal thing. "Yes."

He arched a brow, surprised. "When?"

"Recently. Most of the time."

A slow smile curved his lips. "You don't say?"

Now she wished she hadn't said. She wasn't sure it was cool, letting a man know you wanted him.

"And how did Carmichael fit into this? The last time we were here you insisted I give you some ideas about how to make him want you."

JoJo leaned back on a pillow and stared into the fire that blazed and sent warmth all through her. She then shifted her gaze to Stern, knowing he was waiting for her response. She nibbled on her bottom lip again. "It's complicated, Stern, and I'd rather not go into details. All you need to know is that I thought he was someone I wanted to get to know and I was wrong."

He stared at her for a long moment and she could imagine what he was thinking. He probably assumed she was fickle and shifted her interest from one man to another at the drop of a hat. But to tell him the truth— that she loved him when he didn't love her back—would make her feel pathetic. For him to commit to become her lover was one thing, but for him to find out she loved him might make him run in the other direction.

"Like I told you before, I recently figured out that the reason I enjoyed our kisses so much is because I was becoming attracted to you."

"Wow," JoJo said, smiling. "It still feels nice to hear that. I was becoming attracted to you, too, so this best friends with benefits thing would have happened between us eventually."

Stern wasn't so sure about that. He wanted to believe that eventually their attraction would have prompted them to note the change in their emotions and then to decide to become lovers with a strong commitment, with a future that included marriage.

"So, do we get to sleep together tonight?"

He heard both anxiousness and nervousness in her voice. "No. I want you to think about everything and give me your answer tomorrow. Like I said, I want a commitment. That means becoming a couple in front of everyone. My family and yours. My friends and yours. Everyone. Can you handle that?"

"Yes. They'll think it's strange at first, but I think everyone will be okay with it in the end."

"And if they aren't?"

She lifted her chin. "What we do is our business, right?"

"Right."

He eased to his feet and pulled her up with him. "Let's share a cup of hot chocolate before we go to bed. Think about things tonight and tomorrow you can give me your answer. I don't want you to feel like you're being rushed into anything."

"It was my idea, Stern."

"Doesn't matter. I still want you to be sure."

As he led her into the kitchen, Stern knew it was important to him that JoJo *did* think this through because as far as he was concerned he had their future all mapped out. They would date exclusively for a while and then, when he thought the time was right for both of them, he would pop the question.

He wanted her as his wife. She was an integral part of his past and he couldn't imagine a future without her.

Eleven

Stern was up early the next morning, busy preparing breakfast. Although Mr. Richardson hadn't been able to get the place warm for them on this trip, he had gone grocery shopping, stocking enough food for their weekend visit.

One of Stern's favorite rooms in the lodge was the kitchen. It was huge and spacious and would be a chef's dream. When he had purchased the place he had replaced all the appliances with stainless-steel ones and installed granite countertops. Because the kitchen was so massive, he had an island breakfast bar built, which he used for eating and as an additional countertop.

He had kept the original cherry oak cabinets and he'd let JoJo pick out all the fixtures and the tile for the floor and the backsplash. He had wanted her to feel this place was just as much hers as it was his. At the time, he hadn't thought much about that decision, but now he couldn't help but question it and others he'd made concerning JoJo. No wonder his family had suspected his true feelings for her long before he had.

He had heard JoJo move around upstairs about half an hour ago and was anticipating her joining him for breakfast. Had she given yesterday's request more thought and decided she didn't want the best friends with benefits thing after all? He'd known that encouraging her to think more about it was a risk that might prompt her to change her mind, but he wanted her to be sure she was truly ready for taking such a step.

Last night, before going to bed, they had shared hot chocolate and Danish rolls while he brought her up to date on what was going on with the investigation of his great-grandfather, Raphel Stern Westmoreland.

A few years ago, the family had discovered that Raphel, who they'd always assumed was an only child, had actually had a twin brother, Reginald Scott Westmoreland, who had roots in Atlanta. It seemed Raphel had left home at the age of twenty-two, becoming the black sheep of the family when he ran off with the preacher's wife, never to be heard from again and eventually assumed dead. Raphel had passed through several states before finally settling in Colorado.

It also appeared that his great-grandfather had a colorful past. He'd taken up with several women along the way. Everyone in the family was curious about those women because he was rumored to have married all four.

Recently they had met Reginald's ancestors and had formed a close relationship with those cousins in Atlanta. Now everyone was anxious to see if there were more Westmoreland cousins out there somewhere, resulting from any of those women Raphel had supposedly married.

Rico, Megan's husband, was the private detective handling the investigation. A few months ago, Rico discovered Raphel had a child he hadn't known about. A child who was ultimately adopted by a woman with the last name of Outlaw. And now Rico was investigating information about the woman who was rumored to be Raphel's fourth wife, Isabelle. Just yesterday morning, the family had assembled at Dillon's for breakfast to get an update from Rico. He had informed everyone he was still trying to collect data on Isabelle's family and that he was getting close to obtaining information on the Outlaws. So far he'd traced them to Little Rock and there the trail had ended.

"Good morning."

Stern glanced up from the chopping block and stared at JoJo. Her hair was again styled around her face and she wore a cute maxi sweaterdress that showed off her great shape. It was mint-green and made her look soft, totally feminine and sexy as hell. The material hugged her hips, cushioned her breasts and emphasized her waistline. He definitely liked the cowl-neck collar that bared a little skin. Instead of her boots she had leather flats on her feet. He thought she looked amazing. Gorgeous. Hot. The dress was one that would be easy to slide into and out of. He definitely wouldn't mind seeing her slide out of it.

"Good morning, JoJo. Did you get a good night's sleep?" he asked, trying to control the desire rushing through his bloodstream.

She'd come to stand in the middle of the kitchen. "Yes. After sleeping on the drive here, I figured I would stay awake most of the night, but I didn't. I think I went to sleep as soon as my head touched the pillow."

Did that mean she hadn't thought any more about her proposal? "Glad to hear it. I'm chopping up everything for the omelets. Have a seat at the breakfast bar. I should be finished in a minute."

"Okay."

He watched her walk off, noticing how the wool clung to her shapely backside. And when she eased onto the breakfast bar stool the hem of her dress inched up and showed off a gorgeous pair of legs. Seeing her wear something other than a T-shirt and jeans would take some getting used to.

"About what we discussed last night, Stern…"

He shifted his gaze from her legs to her face. His gut tightened. "Yes?"

"I did sleep on it, and I haven't changed my mind."

He released a slow, relieved breath. "Okay."

The kitchen quieted for a moment and then she asked, "Need help?"

"Nope." He went back to slicing the green peppers.

That's usually how things went with them. He would end up in the kitchen because he liked cooking more than she did. She would ask if he needed help and he would decline. Nothing had changed. But in reality things *had* changed. Now the air between them was charged, explosive, volatile. Desire thickened inside of him each and every time he glanced over at her. It wouldn't take much to cross the room and…

"So what's for breakfast in addition to the omelet?"

He glanced up from the ingredients. "The usual— French toast, fruit, orange juice and coffee."

"Can you add something else to the menu?"

"Sure. What?"

"You."

Stern held her gaze for the longest moment. Every pore in his body filled with a degree of hunger he'd never felt before. A fire burned inside of him, spreading fast and furious through his veins. For the first time in his life, a woman had him sizzling. He gathered all the sliced vegetables in the palms of his hands and dropped them in a bowl. Taking a couple of steps back, he placed the bowl in the refrigerator.

After wiping his hands on a kitchen towel, he slowly crossed the room toward her. "I had planned a picnic for us later today, and then I figured we would have movie night. I'd even selected several DVDs for us to watch." Coming to a stop in front of her, he lifted her off the bar stool to stand in front of him. "I didn't want to rush you. I wanted to court you first."

"That's not necessary," she said, leaning her body into his. "I know what I want. Before today, I figured having that particular want was an impossibility. However, I woke up this morning knowing I could finally have what I desire."

He thought she had a way with words and for the next few hours he intended to lap any and all of them from her lips. Starting now. He leaned down and painted feather-light kisses around her mouth, then he licked around the edges of her lips with the tip of his tongue before nibbling around her ear.

"I think it's time for us to take this to the bedroom," he said huskily. Then he swept her off her feet and into his arms.

JoJo wondered how Stern managed to carry her up the stairs as if she weighed no more than a child. Wrapped in his arms, with her ear pressed against his chest, she heard the erratic beat of his heart. She felt his desire and it fed her own.

She'd woken up that morning feeling happier than she had in a long time. Although Stern hadn't said he loved her, he did say he wanted her, his best friend, and he wanted her the same way she wanted him. For her, that was a start.

JoJo felt the mattress beneath her when he placed her on the bed. He stepped back and she held tight to the gaze of the one man who knew her better than anyone else. The one man who'd shared her happiness and her sorrows. He had been her protector, her confidant and, when she needed it, her critic. He'd encouraged her to follow her dreams and had been there to tell her when she'd gotten in too far over her head. She had loved him as her best friend—in fact, she still did. But now she also loved him as the one man who could make her feel complete.

He moved toward the bed, placed his knee on the mattress and tenderly stroked her cheek. "Last chance."

She knew what he meant. "Thanks, but I'm not taking it," she whispered, still holding his gaze.

"You've thought this through, then?"

"Very much so. I want you," she whispered.

"And I want you."

He pulled her into his arms and took her mouth with a passion that plunged her senses into overload. The way his tongue devoured hers created a torrid storm within her that made her moan deep in her throat.

He pulled away and she felt air touch her skin as he whisked her dress over her head, leaving her wearing only her thong.

"Ah, hell." Stern felt his guts twist into knots as his gaze raked over JoJo. *Heaven help me.* She was perfect. Long graceful neck, firm breasts, beautiful skin and an adorable flat stomach.

This would be her first time with a man, and he wanted to be gentle. He wanted to take it slow, make it last, make it good and keep it mellow. But seeing her nearly naked, wearing just a tiny scrap of a thong, was more than he could handle. The sight made him want to take her hard and fast, but he knew there was no way he could. He would never hurt her.

Fighting for control, he said softly, "Lie back and lift your hips for me. I want to take this last piece off of you."

She followed his request and he slid the thong over her hips and down her legs. His fingers trembled when they came in contact with her soft skin. He caught a whiff of her feminine scent and he hardened even more, pressing against the zipper of his jeans.

When she lay completely naked before him, he knew he'd never seen a body as beautiful as hers. Unable to fight temptation, he leaned toward her, his greedy mouth targeting her nipples.

He sucked, nibbled and licked to his heart's content. And his hands, of their own accord, drifted slowly down her body, touching her waist, running circles around her belly button and moving even lower, toward the essence of her heat.

When he touched her womanly core, she tried to close her legs on his hands in surprise. "Let me, baby," he said softly, lifting his face from her breasts to gaze up at her. Using his hands, he reopened her legs, spreading them wide.

She moaned when he slid two fingers inside her wet center. He held her gaze as he stroked her, needing to see the play of emotions on her face. Pleasuring a woman had never meant so much to him and he loved the way her eyes dilated, the way her lips parted on breathless moans, the way flames of passion spread across her cheeks.

His fingers moved inside her swiftly, thoroughly. When her inner muscles clamped tight, he deepened his strokes until he couldn't take any more. Her womanly scent aroused him. He had to taste her. He wouldn't be satisfied until his tongue delved into heated bliss.

"Enjoy," he whispered, before shifting his body and lowering his head between her legs. She tensed but his mouth quickly replaced his fingers and he gripped her hips to keep her steady. He swirled his tongue inside of her, loving her taste, loving the sounds of her lusty moans.

"Stern!"

Her body quivered beneath his mouth but he wouldn't let up or let go. He intended this day to be one of never-ending pleasure for her. It would be one he didn't ever want her to forget.

JoJo was convinced she was dying and Stern's mouth was to blame. All sorts of sensations shot through her, but she felt them mostly right beneath his mouth. He kept kissing her there, using his tongue to do all kinds of wicked things to her.

She was loving it.

She closed her eyes and lifted her hips, brazenly wanting more. Never in a million years would she have seen herself behaving this way. It was as if he had brought out something wild and untamed inside of her and all she could do was...*enjoy*...just like he'd told her to do.

Then she felt something building inside of her, a stirring pressure in her belly and even more erotic sensations where he kissed her. Then he did something with his tongue—she wasn't sure what—but she felt it all the way to her womb. Her body bucked and that building sensation exploded. She screamed his name, clenching his head and trying to clutch his shoulders. It seemed as if that overwhelming sensation had broken into fragments that she felt in every bone, every pore, every part of her.

Her body felt like molten liquid. She breathed his name, convinced she had died and accepting that if she

had died then it had been a damn good death. If she had
to go, this was the way to do it.

Even when he had removed his mouth from her, she
lay there. She was too weak to even open her eyes, lift her
hand, close her legs. She had to force herself to breathe,
slowly and deeply.

"JoJo."

In the deep recesses of her mind she heard Stern's
voice. With all the strength she could muster, she opened
her eyes, one at a time. Then she widened her gaze when
she saw he was removing his shirt.

Surely he didn't think she was up for anything else
after that amazing experience. She would need an entire
day to recuperate. Maybe two days. Possibly three. She
was new at this and he had to know there was no way
her body could rejuvenate itself this soon.

"Stern?" she called out when she heard him sliding
down his zipper.

"Yes, baby?"

"I can't move." Hopefully that would tell him something. Evidently it didn't. He kept removing his clothes
and was now easing his jeans down his legs, followed
by his briefs. And then she saw him. Oh, boy did she
see him. She had to widen her eyes to make sure what
she was seeing was real and not an illusion. Was it even
possible?

That's when something unexpected happened. A stirring spread through her. Her nipples hardened, her belly
quivered and the juncture of her legs began to throb. She
was zapped with renewed energy and she couldn't fathom
the source. All she knew was that suddenly she had the
strength to move her body. She eased up on her haunches.

"I thought you couldn't move."

A smooth smile touched the corner of his lips. He'd

known her body would come back to life. Of course he'd known. He was a pro at this. He'd known her body would blaze with desire all over again just by looking at him.

"I wanted to make sure I wasn't seeing things," she said, staring at what she knew was probably every woman's fantasy. But she was trying desperately to figure out how this was going to go down.

He evidently saw the deep concentration on her face. "It will be okay, trust me," he said softly.

She hoped so because her body was already affected by what she saw. Streaks of desire, tugs of sexual urges, patches of warmth began to consume her, seeming to touch every inch of her body, even those places she figured should still be recovering from her orgasm.

"Are you still on the Pill?"

She looked up into his eyes. "Yes."

There was no need to ask him how he knew. He'd picked up her prescription once or twice when she'd been ill. He also knew why the doctor had prescribed them for her. More than once Stern had held her hand when painful cramps had forced her into bed.

"I can still use a condom," he offered.

She tilted her head to study him once more below the waist. He was probably used to doing so, but it couldn't really be easy. "That's not necessary."

"You sure?"

She was certain she wanted to go through with this, but she still wasn't convinced it would work. "Yes, I'm sure."

"In that case." He slowly moved toward the bed, and she watched him, fascinated and nervous at the same time. He had a powerful stride, a magnificent body. He was definitely an alpha male. He watched her watching him and by sheer willpower alone her breath came from her lungs evenly. He had the physique of masculine physiques—tight abs, nice solid chest—but what held her attention was the engorged erection nested in a thick bed of curly hair.

Who would have thought Stern would one day have this kind of effect on her? She'd often wondered how her first time would be and with whom. Who would have thought that he would be the one? But he was, and she couldn't be happier. That's why a smile touched her lips.

When he reached the bed, she eased up on her knees and extended her arms out to him. And when he pulled her against that hard chest, she met his gaze and knew this was right. This was how it should be.

Capturing her mouth with his, he lowered them both to the bed. She should be familiar with his kisses by now, but she wasn't. She was a firm believer in his ability to design a kiss to give maximum pleasure. He kissed her deeply, thoroughly, taking possession and staking a claim.

Her fingers dug into his shoulders. The feel of her breasts pressed against his chest electrified every single cell in her body. Every kiss was better than the last. Her mouth had been made just for his.

He released her mouth only to begin kissing the side of her face and neck. And she knew the exact moment when he added his hands to the mix. His strokes on her thigh felt purely sensual. She closed her eyes as intense pleasure eased up her body. And when his mouth moved from her neck to her breasts, licking, sucking and nibbling, flames rushed through her.

His hands eased between her legs and she moaned out his name. "I want you, JoJo. I want you," he whispered. "You're wet and ready."

He eased up and slid his entire body over hers while

still gazing down at her. His hands entangled with hers by the sides of her face. And then she felt it—his engorged erection pressing against her womanhood. His gaze remained locked with hers as he slowly slid inside of her, inch by incredible inch, and, amazingly, her body stretched to accommodate him.

"Just a little more to go," he whispered.

Sensations concentrated right there, where their bodies were connected. She tightened her inner muscles around him. "Ah, hell," he said, thrusting hard inside her, making her suck in a deep gasp of surprise.

"You okay?" he asked, looking down at her.

She felt him. He was in. All the way. Astonishing. "Yes, I'm okay." She was elated.

He then began moving, with slow, powerful thrusts that stimulated her in a way she'd never been stimulated before. His movements fueled her desire, created needs she'd never encountered, encouraged her to take what he was offering.

He lengthened his strokes. He went deeper and her inner muscles clamped down even more. He let go of her hands and gripped her hips, increasing his pace, establishing a rhythm that nearly pushed her over the edge.

JoJo gripped the bedspread as he began thrusting harder, going deeper. She moaned out his name as sensations whisked through her, withdrawing and then going back in again.

"Stern!"

She screamed his name and clutched his shoulders, lifting her hips to meet his. Over and over and over... then he bucked, threw back his head and growled her name. Her body exploded at the same time that his did. She seized his hips to hold him right where she needed him and she felt his release inside of her.

"JoJo!"

"Stern!"

And as their bodies stilled, he kissed her in an exchange that was bittersweet, passionate and intimate all rolled into one.

She knew she could never love him any more than she did at that very moment.

Twelve

To Stern's way of thinking, nothing hit the spot like good food, fine wine and a beautiful woman. And this evening he was enjoying all three. The sun was going down over the mountains and the trees reflected the autumn leaves in aspen gold, brilliant yellow and tinges of orange and red. From the deck, the sight was picturesque. Scenic. Vivid.

He shifted his gaze to JoJo. How would he describe her? Beautiful. Striking. Sexy. Yes, definitely sexy. She sat in the chair, sipping her wine and watching the view. She was wearing another dress, this one in a paisley pattern. He appreciated the low-cut neckline and how the shirred crossover bodice complemented her breasts. She looked as hot as she had earlier that morning in the kitchen.

The lower part of his body throbbed when he remembered the morning. After making love, they'd dozed off, waking up right before lunch to eat the breakfast they should have eaten earlier. Starving, they'd devoured the omelets with French toast, juice and coffee, then ravenous for each other again they'd gone back to bed and stayed there until their stomachs had sent another signal it was time to be fed.

They'd gotten up and showered together. He had grilled a couple of steaks and she had prepared the salad, selected the wine and set the table on the deck. It was a little chilly so he'd fired up the fire pit he'd had built on the deck for days just like this. The heat from the pit warmed them and made being outside enjoyable.

"It's hard to believe it's been a week."

He took a sip of his wine and glanced over at her. "A week?"

"Yes, since my makeover."

Yes, it had been a week and he doubted he would ever forget how she'd looked when she'd walked into the Punch Bowl. "So other than Carmichael calling to say he wanted his auto records transferred, you haven't heard from him?"

"No, and I don't expect to, either. He found out the hard way that he didn't impress me. I still find it hard to believe that he acted the way he did."

Stern didn't find it hard to believe, especially after what Sampson had shared with him. "So tell me. Do I impress you?"

She looked at him and smiled. "Yes, you impress me."

He reached over and touched her arm, liking the feel of her soft skin. "You impress me, too."

At that moment, he considered telling her he loved her, but he knew it was too soon. He needed to give her time. Give them time to become a couple. He thought of how often they'd shared an afternoon on the deck like this. But tonight things were different. They were officially lovers. And one day they would be husband and wife.

"Thanks for being patient with me today."

He chuckled. "You must have me mixed up with someone else. I don't recall being patient. In fact, I almost ripped your dress off."

She chuckled. "You whipped it over my head before I even realized you were doing it. You have such practiced hands."

Stern thought about all the women he'd hooked up with over the years. His numbers weren't as outlandish as Riley's, Zane's or Derringer's, so he'd never really thought of himself as a ladies' man. He'd always been just a guy out for fun. He'd dated, never lied to a woman about his intentions and kept moving on.

He had enjoyed being single, had preferred not having to answer to anyone. He had actually cringed when the die-hard bachelors in his family got married.

Derringer had been the first a few years ago when he'd married Lucia, and now Derringer had settled down to the role of father and husband rather nicely. Riley was getting married at the end of the month and Zane over the Christmas holidays. Stern had understood Canyon's quick wedding last month because there had been a child involved, but for his other relatives, he just couldn't figure why any man would willingly give up his single status.

Now he did.

Once you'd fallen in love everything else became secondary to the woman you desired above all else. Thanks to her father, JoJo was independent, and Stern had always admired that streak in her. He still did. But he wondered how she would adjust now that he was more than her best friend, now that he wanted to be more than her lover? How would she feel about him as a possible husband?

"So, what movie did you pick out for us?" she asked, breaking into his thoughts.

He glanced up. She had stood and was gathering their

dishes. His body stirred. Why was he reacting to her every time she moved? "What do you suggest? You know the kind that I prefer."

"And you know the kind I like," she countered.

Yes, he knew the kind. Once in a while he appeased her by watching some chick flick and then he normally fell asleep at some point before it was over. "We could play cards," he suggested. "Or chess."

"We played those the last time we were here. Where's that Scrabble game? We haven't played that in a while."

"And I don't want to work my brain to play it now." An idea came into his head. "I know a game I'm sure we haven't played in years. It's usually played with a group, but it should be interesting with just the two of us."

"What game is that?"

"Simon Says."

She gave him an incredulous look. "Simon Says?"

"Yes." She scrunched her forehead, giving his suggestion some thought. "How do we decide who gets to be Simon?"

"We can toss a coin. The rules are as follows. If you get to be Simon and can make me follow a command that's not Simon's, then I will be at your beck and call for the rest of the night. If you can't, then you will be at my beck and call."

"Beck and call?" she asked, raising a brow.

"Yes, beck and call."

She gave him a slow smile as if the idea appealed to her. Evidently she saw a lot of possibilities in his suggestion. "And just how many commands are we talking about?"

"No more than twenty."

She nodded slowly before saying, "Okay, that will

work. Let me take these dishes into the kitchen and then we can meet in the living room. Just be ready."

Stern smiled. He would definitely be ready.

Stern won the coin toss and JoJo would have thought it was rigged if she hadn't been the one who'd tossed the coin. On top of letting her toss, he'd been nice enough to let her pick heads or tails. She would be hard-pressed to make the claim that something wasn't aboveboard.

So here she was, standing in the middle of the floor, waiting for Stern to issue the first command. She hadn't played this game in years and wondered what possessed him to think of it, although a part of her had an idea. In fact, with him standing a few feet in front of her with a silly grin on his face, she had more than an idea.

"Oh, yeah," he said as his smile deepened. "As in most Simon Says games, there is no talking. Just follow the command like you're supposed to, but only if Simon says you can."

"Whatever."

"All right, let's get started. Simon says hold up your right hand."

She followed that command.

"Put it down."

She kept her hand up. If he thought he was going to catch her with that one, he had another think coming.

"Simon says put it down."

She put her hand down.

"Put it back up."

She kept it down.

He smiled. She smiled back.

"Simon says stand on one leg."

She followed his command.

"Simon says go around once in a circle."

She frowned at him because it wasn't easy maneuvering that command and she had a feeling he knew it. She went around once in a circle.

"Simon says you can put your leg down."

She did.

"Put it back up."

She didn't. JoJo wasn't sure if he was keeping count but she was. So far he'd issued eight commands and she was still in the game. Twelve more to go and she would be home free. Already her mind was buzzing with the things she could have him do. Painting her toenails sounded pretty good.

"Simon says take off your clothes."

Her head jerked in his direction and she frowned. She had known he was up to no good. Just as she parted her lips to say something, he quickly spoke up. "Remember, if you talk you forfeit the game."

JoJo closed her mouth and frowned some more, thinking that he would pay dearly for this. When she was declared winner and he was at her beck and call, she'd not only make him paint her nails, she would also have him go out in the cold without a shirt and collect more firewood.

"Simon says he doesn't have all day," he said, grinning. "So I repeat, Simon says take off your clothes."

Glaring, she slowly eased down her side zipper before tugging the dress over her head. That left her standing in front of him wearing only her tangerine-colored bra and matching panties. If his intent had been to get her naked, why hadn't he just suggested strip poker?

"Nice," he said, raking his gaze over her. The heated look in his eyes warmed her body. Now she was glad that his girl cousins and sisters-in-law had talked her into getting rid of her white panties and bras and buying colorful matching sets.

"Simon says remove your bra and panties."

After removing her bra, she eased her panties down her legs.

"Slowly lick your bottom lip."

JoJo caught herself in time before doing that command. This was a mind game and she had to stay focused on what Stern was saying and not on how he was looking at her while she stood before him wearing not a stitch of clothes. She'd never felt this exposed, this vulnerable. Even when they'd made love earlier she had stayed under the covers, while he'd walked around the room unashamedly showing himself. Had he detected her uneasiness regarding putting her body on display?

Stern drew in a deep breath as a knot of desire tightened his chest. Heat sizzled through his veins, making his erection throb. Never had he seen such a beautifully made woman and he had known, when they made love, that she had a problem showing her body.

Oh, he'd seen the tiny scar on the side of her hip, the one she'd gotten when she'd fallen off her skateboard at the age of fourteen. And then there was the sister scar from the same accident, located above it, near her waist. They weren't noticeable unless attention was drawn to them. Little did she know he thought she was exquisite. Perfect in every aspect. He wanted to show her that he could stand there and stare at her all day…even while his body was getting more aroused by the second.

"Come here."

When she didn't move, a slow smile touched his lips. He then said, "Simon says come here."

She slowly walked toward him. When she came to

a stop within a foot of him, he said, "Simon says undress me."

She stared at him for a minute before pulling his sweater over his head. Then she eased his belt through the loops before removing it completely and tossing it aside. Next was his jeans. She slowly eased down his zipper before crouching down to tug the pants, along with his briefs, down his legs. Lucky for her, he had removed his shoes earlier so all he had to do was step out of his jeans when she had worked them past his knees to his ankles.

Before standing back on her feet she was face-to-face with the swollen length of him. He hadn't planned to give the next command, but when she glanced up at him and he'd seen the clash of desire and curiosity in her gaze, he said in a husky tone, "Simon says taste it."

A smile touched her mouth before she parted her lips and slid him deep inside. He thought he would drop to his knees in pleasure. Instead, he threw his head back and released a guttural growl. His hands grabbed a fistful of her hair while she tasted him in a way no one ever had. Her curiosity made her bold, audacious and confident as she used her tongue to explore every single inch of him.

He was close, too close, and their game would be over before he had a chance to finish all his commands. Tightening his hold on her head, he uttered thickly, "JoJo, stop."

When she kept right on with her torture he recalled what he needed to say. "Simon says stop."

She slid her mouth off him and stood to her feet with a satisfied grin. He inwardly chuckled. She knew exactly what she'd been doing, the little vixen. But he had no complaints.

He studied her as she stood in front of him, waiting for Simon's next command. She had no idea just how much he loved her, adored her. He intended to do everything within his power to make her realize just how much he wanted her to be a part of his life forever.

He grabbed one of the chairs from a nearby table and sat down. He glanced up at her. "Simon says straddle me."

She slowly eased her body into his lap, straddling his thighs. The warmth of her skin touched his and he breathed in her scent. He held her gaze as they sat face-to-face. "Simon says to take me inside of you."

She lifted her hips and shifted a little. He moaned when he felt his engorged shaft penetrating her wet flesh and he slid slowly inside of her. He had one more command left and he intended to make it last. It didn't matter that she'd won the game. All that mattered was that in the end they'd both get what they wanted.

He licked the side of her face right beneath her ear and whispered, "Simon says ride me hard."

She obeyed the command at once, rotating her hips, pumping on him. He drew in a sharp breath when she grabbed his shoulders and showed him just what her body could do.

He buried his face between her breasts before tilting his head to the side to take a nipple into his mouth. He grabbed her thighs as she gyrated her hips, her inner muscles clenching him. When he felt her body explode and she screamed his name, he tightened his hold on her, screamed her name and let the essence of his release blast off inside of her.

"JoJo!"

He thrust deep within her, exploding inside her a second time as sensations rushed through him. She trembled in his arms and he knew he was trembling, too. As their breathing slowly returned to normal, he held her in his arms. He needed the feel of her, chest to chest, hearts connected.

Stern whispered, "We need to take this to the bedroom, don't you think?"

She chuckled against the side of his face. "As long as you remember that, for the rest of the night, you're at my beck and call."

He drew in a deep breath. "I have no problem with that, sweetheart. No problem at all."

Thirteen

If anyone had asked, JoJo would have admitted that her life over the past few weeks had been perfect. While at the lodge, she and Stern decided they deserved another day and instead of leaving on Sunday, they'd left Monday evening, arriving back at her place before midnight.

He had spent the night at her place, and then she'd spent a night at his place. They'd been inseparable practically every night since, when he wasn't traveling.

She would also admit that making the transition from best friends to lovers had its perks. With him, she could be herself, the JoJo she'd always been. And she could also discover who else she wanted to be. She'd found she could be brazen, shamelessly so, and, at times, Stern would blatantly egg her on. She totally and thoroughly enjoyed it when he did.

It was hard to believe two weeks had passed since their decision to become best friends with benefits. Tonight, he was taking her to a fund-raising dinner for heart research, and she was happy about going with him. They'd gone out to dinner a few times, attended movies and football games, but this would be the first evening where they would be seen together at a public event as a couple. She was rather nervous about it.

Which was why she'd looked at herself in the mirror a dozen times since she'd finished dressing. She loved her gown and thought she looked striking in it. Stern had picked it out and purchased it for her. She had been surprised and elated when she had received the huge box.

When she'd pulled out the very flattering white gown, she'd been in awe. The dress gave the illusion that the person wearing it was a goddess. Silver beads ran the length of the gown but were only visible when she walked. It definitely made a stunning statement and the feel of the soft georgette on her skin was fabulous. And to think that he'd known her body measurements to a tee!

Really, she should not be surprised. He seemed to love touching her. He would spend time just running his hands all over her body, and she loved when he did it. Her independent side had made her offer to pay him for the gown, but he would not hear of it, telling her to consider it an early birthday present. And because her birthday was next month, she had conceded.

Her heart jumped when she heard her doorbell and she couldn't stop the smile that broke out on her face. After looking in the mirror one last time, she grabbed her purse off the table and moved toward the door.

The man she loved had arrived.

Aiden Westmoreland glanced over at his cousin. "JoJo looks simply breathtaking tonight, Stern."

Stern nodded, refusing to let his gaze leave JoJo as she danced around the ballroom with Derringer. "Thanks. Yes, she does."

He'd been in Los Angeles on business and had spotted it in the window in a boutique in Beverly Hills. As far as he was concerned, JoJo's name had been written all over it so he'd bought it for her.

"So what's going on with you, Aiden?" His cousin was the newest doctor in the family and had decided to do his residency at a hospital in Maine.

"Nothing, just hard at work. I needed this break."

"Did you?" Stern asked, taking a sip of his wine as he studied his cousin. He could remember when Aiden and his identical twin, Adrian, and their sister Bailey and Stern's brother Bane, were the terror of Denver. "So your being home has nothing to do with the fact that Jillian decided to come home this weekend, too?"

Stern inwardly chuckled when Aiden almost choked on his wine. He gave his cousin a couple of whacks on the back. "Wine go down the wrong pipe, Aiden?"

Aiden glared at him. "Did you have to hit me on the back so hard?"

"Yes, I thought it would knock some sense into you. I hope you know what you're doing with Jill. If you're trying to mess her over, then—"

"What do you think you know about me and Jill?"

"Only what I saw the last time you were home. I was out riding Legend Boy that morning you were supposed to take Jill to the airport. From what I'd heard from Pam, Jill was supposed to be there at five in the morning, which is why you had volunteered to take her. So I'm sure you can imagine my surprise when I saw you whip Jillian out of the car and into your arms that morning and carry her into Gemma's house." Gemma's house stood empty because she had married and moved to Australia.

"It's not what you think," Aiden said in his defense.

"I'm not the one you need to be telling that to. All I've got to say is that you'd better hope Pam and Dil don't find out what you're up to."

"I love her."

"Then why the sneaking around?"

Aiden didn't say anything for a moment. "You know Pam's plan for Jill. After she finishes medical school in the spring, Pam hopes she'll—"

"What does Jill want?" Stern interrupted to ask.

Aiden didn't say anything for a moment and then he responded, "She wants us to be together but doesn't want to disappoint Pam."

Stern shrugged. "Either way, the two of you should come clean and let everyone know how you feel."

"Like you've come clean and let everyone know how you feel about JoJo? I don't see you standing on the highest rooftop shouting out anything."

Aiden's words stirred Stern's gut because what his cousin had said was true. He hadn't told anyone how he really felt about JoJo, not even JoJo, but then most who truly knew him were probably well aware that he was a man purely smitten. But still...

"Sorry, I shouldn't have said that, man," Aiden said. "Everyone in the family knows how crazy you are about JoJo. Look over me tonight. I'm in a bad mood about Jill right now because we argued earlier. I want to go to Dil and Pam and tell them the truth, but she's against it. And that bothers me more than anything. I don't like deceiving them, but I'm doing it anyway."

"It sounds like you and Jill need to make some decisions."

And it seemed, Stern thought, that he needed to make some decisions, too.

* * *

JoJo strolled out of the ladies' room and walked right into someone blocking her way.

"Well, well, if it isn't the grease lady. You can take the woman out of the auto repair shop but you can never really get the grease off the lady. I'm sure there's grease somewhere on that body of yours."

Anger sliced through her. His insulting words were deserving of a slap to the face, but she refused to make a scene tonight like she'd done at the Punch Bowl. Besides, Walter Carmichael wasn't worth it. Deciding to ignore him and move on, she tried to walk past him. He reached out and grabbed her arm with force, jerking her to him.

"You embarrassed me that night at the Punch Bowl and you also straight out lied about your relationship with Westmoreland. Best friends, my ass. There's more going on between you two—anyone can see that. And I'm going to make sure you pay for being a tease."

"Get your hands off me before I knock your eyeballs out of their sockets."

He immediately let her go and she quickly walked off without looking back. She tried not to fume, but Walter had her riled. When she reentered the ballroom, she met Stern heading toward her.

"You okay?" he asked her in a voice filled with anger. She studied his features. "Yes, why wouldn't I be?"

"Lucia said she saw a man grab for you when you came out of the ladies' room. I figured it was Carmichael since I saw him earlier. What did he say? What did he want?"

She thought about mentioning the threat Walter had made but decided against it. The man was all bluster, and the last thing she wanted was to ruin Stern's night like Walter had tried to ruin hers. Besides, she had handled it.

"Nothing and nothing. At least nothing worth mentioning. I shut him down. It's okay."

"It's not okay. If he manhandled you, then—"

"I took care of it," she said. "I don't need you handling my business."

He stared at her for a long minute and then asked softly, "Has it ever occurred to you that your business is my business?"

She shrugged. "No, because I don't recall that being part of the deal when it comes to being best friends with benefits."

"Then maybe we need to discuss just what our relationship entails," he said.

JoJo detected anger in his voice, and she couldn't understand why. Was Stern missing his role of ladies' man? He didn't seem to be, but she couldn't help but wonder, especially when she saw women vying for his attention. He'd always said that he enjoyed the chase.

She would admit she was a little annoyed at the number of women who had tried to make a pass at him tonight. Some so brazen it was ridiculous, going so far as to approach him as if JoJo wasn't there. Maybe some of them assumed she and Stern were still nothing more than best friends, but even when he'd placed his arms around her waist in a more intimate gesture and introduced her as his date, most gave her a haughty look as if to say, "Good luck trying to hold on to him."

"JoJo, are you listening to what I said?"

Honestly, she hadn't been. She did recall he'd said something about them needing to discuss what their relationship entailed. "If you think we need to talk, fine. But when it comes to Walter Carmichael, I can handle myself. I don't need you to fight my battles."

She then walked off.

* * *

Somehow Stern held his anger in check for the rest of the night, but he couldn't help noticing that things between him and JoJo were strained. She barely said anything on the drive home.

As soon as the door closed behind them at her place, he knew they had to talk. "What's bothering you, JoJo?"

She looked at him with fire flashing in her eyes. "Nothing's wrong with me other than the fact that you have some brazen ex-girlfriends. I've never met women so disrespectful."

He was well aware that jealousy had driven a few of those women tonight. They'd wanted to get a rise out of her. "I hope you didn't let their behavior get to you. When I saw what they were doing I did set them straight, didn't I?"

"Yes, you did, but…"

"But what?"

"Nothing."

He crossed his arms over his chest. "You've used that word a lot tonight, don't you think? And I know you. When you say 'nothing,' most of the time there is something. So come on, let's talk."

He tugged her over to the sofa and into his lap. "Now tell me."

She didn't say anything for a moment. "Before, you liked women. Lots of women. And you enjoyed the chase. Now you're stuck with dull little me. You must miss your old lifestyle."

Stern looked at her for a long moment, knowing she didn't have a clue. What she'd just said didn't come close to being factual. So maybe it was time he told her the truth. "I love you, JoJo."

She waved off his words. "Of course you love me and

I love you, which is why we've put up with each other all these years and—"

He placed a hand over her mouth to stop her from talking. "Listen to what I'm saying for a second. I love you. I love you the way a man and a woman love each other."

Stern was certain JoJo would have fallen out of his lap if he hadn't been holding her so tightly. Her eyes widened and her mouth dropped open as she stared at him. She then shook her head. "No, you can't love me that way."

"Why can't I?"

"Because that's the way I love you."

Now it was Stern's turn to be stumped, and he was speechless. He shifted JoJo's position so they were facing each other. He wanted to look into her face while they were talking. "Are you saying that you're in love with me...the same way I'm in love with you?" he asked her.

She shrugged. "I don't know. What way are you in love with me?"

He knew she hadn't asked to be funny but truly wanted to know. "I'm in love with you in the way where I think of you all the time, even when I'm at work. In the way where I think I smell you even when you aren't there. I'm in love with you in the way where you are the first person on my mind when I wake up in the morning and the last person on my mind before going to bed at night. In the way where having sex is now making love. And in the way where whenever I'm inside of you I want to go deeper and deeper because I want to be consumed by you and you by me. No matter what, I will always be here for you, even during those times when I know you can take care of yourself. Loving you makes me want to take care of you anyway."

JoJo had tears in her eyes. "I've never heard a declaration of love stated so beautifully." She swallowed. "When did you know?"

"To be honest with you, I'm not sure. I might have loved you forever. My family suspected I did, but it's only been revealed to me lately. Your fascination with Carmichael made me realize what you meant to me."

She nibbled on her bottom lip and then said, "I was only fascinated with Walter because of you. I thought I needed him."

Stern lifted a brow. "I don't understand. What do you mean? You needed him for what?"

He tensed and she wrapped her arms around his neck. "I noticed I was becoming attracted to you when we were together at the lodge in the spring. It was more than attraction, really. I knew I had fallen in love with you and it scared me because I'd never been attracted to a man before…and especially not to you. You were my best friend, and I couldn't fall in love with my best friend. So I came up with what I thought would be the perfect plan."

"Which was?"

"To find someone else to fall in love with."

A smile touched Stern's lips. "I don't think it works that way, JoJo."

"That's what I found out."

Stern didn't say anything for a moment. "So are you telling me that this whole Carmichael thing was a plan you concocted because you'd fallen in love with me and were trying to fight it by trying to fall in love with another man?"

"Yes. Sounds crazy, huh?"

Stern chuckled. "No crazier than the fact that I've been denying loving you, even when Zane called me out on it."

"He did?"

"Yes, more than once. Riley called me out on it, as

well. You and I did admit at the lodge that we were attracted to each other, but what we should have done was come clean with our true feelings."

"Yes, we should have. So let's do it now. Stern, I love you as my best friend, my lover and the man I will always want in my life."

A smile curved his lips. "And Jovonnie 'JoJo' Jones, I love you as my best friend, my lover and the woman I will always want in my life."

"Oh, Stern, I was afraid if you found out how I felt that I could lose you altogether. And with all your brothers and cousins getting married, I was worried about you falling in love and that woman not accepting our close relationship and forcing you to cool things between us."

He nodded. "That crossed my mind, too, when you seemed so obsessed with Carmichael. I was afraid he would come between our friendship, and I couldn't let that happen."

Both of them were quiet for a few moments and then Stern said, "I wish I had leveled with you about my feelings before now, but maybe things happened as they should have for us."

She stared at him. "You mean becoming best friends with benefits?"

"Yes. But now we know the truth. What I need you to understand is that loving someone means caring for that person, comforting that person, being their protector and their strength whenever they need it. I know all of your skills as a marksman, a karate champ and an archer, but that doesn't eliminate my desire to look after you. To want to protect you. And those times that I do want to protect you, just humor me, okay."

She smiled. "Okay."

He then leaned forward and kissed her with a hunger

and need he felt throughout his body. The connection with her was different now because he knew how she felt and she knew how he felt. When she quivered in his arms, he tightened his hands around her waist.

Moments later, he pulled back and forced air into his lungs before taking her mouth again in a kiss that was hungrier than before. Then, suddenly, the need to make love to her was fierce. Intense. Extreme. Powerful.

Stern stood up from the sofa with her in his arms. His destination was the bedroom upstairs, but he only made it to the wall near the staircase and pressed her against it. "I can't go any farther," he moaned, taking her lips again.

He put his hands everywhere, but mostly underneath her gown. When he'd first seen the gown he'd liked it, but now there was too much of it. He finally found the zipper in the back and with practiced hands slid it down. Then he shifted his body away from her just enough to grip the gown at her shoulders and quickly yank it off her.

He heard her suck in a deep breath. "Stern, can you slow down? You're going to ruin my dress."

"No, I can't slow down and I'll buy you another one."

He went still when he saw what she was wearing beneath her gown. A sexy white lace garter belt set with matching thong and back seam stockings. Stern was convinced he'd never seen anything or anyone so sensual in his entire life. "Nice," he said on a tortured moan.

"I'll be sure to let your cousins and sisters-in-law know how much you appreciate it. Just another thing they talked me into buying when we went shopping earlier this month."

"I'll make sure they take you shopping more often. Now, I'm taking it off you."

"I think that was the idea."

In no time at all, Stern had removed every stitch of

her clothing. Not to be undone, JoJo stripped him naked, too. Beginning with his tux jacket, which she shoved off his shoulders, she removed all his clothes. "Now, we're even."

"If that makes you happy," he said, lifting her off her feet and pressing her back against the wall once more. He smiled up at her. "I so enjoy getting into you."

She returned his smile. "And I so enjoy you getting into me."

With that said, he widened her legs with his knee before sliding his engorged shaft inside her, not stopping until he was as deep as he could get. She felt tight. She felt right.

She wrapped her legs around him as he moved, thrusting, filling her, withdrawing and then filling her again. Over and over. Her scent overwhelmed him, stimulated him, and the feel of her soft skin against his swamped his senses. The sounds of her moans only made his body want more.

He tried to slow down and make it last, but then she'd clamp her inner muscles, overpowering him with sensation. He was close, but he refused to climax without her.

He sucked a breast between his lips. She arched her body in a perfect bow while crying out her pleasure. The heels of her feet dug into his back, her fingernails plowed into his shoulder, but all he could feel was the ecstasy of being inside of her.

And then she screamed his name. His mouth left her breast to claim her lips and there it stayed, even when his body jerked from the force of his own orgasm.

He felt more than just love for her. He adored her, cherished her. He would always and forever honor her.

When he slowly disconnected their bodies and eased her legs down, it was only to lift her back into his arms.

"I think we were headed this way before we got side-tracked," he said, moving up the stairs.

"Getting sidetracked can be a good thing," she whispered, placing kisses on his chest.

When they reached her bedroom, they fell on the mattress together, fully intent on making this a night they would both remember for a long time.

Fourteen

JoJo glanced over at the clock when she got up from her desk to pour another cup of coffee. It was close to ten. It had been a long time since she had worked this late at the shop. But it was the end of the month and paperwork had to be completed. Due to federal regulations regarding hazardous wastes, air emissions and wastewater, she had a ton of reports to finalize. It seemed there were more this month than the last. Wanda had stayed as late as seven, but she had a date with her ex and had to leave.

Stretching her body, JoJo took a sip of coffee. It wasn't as good as Stern's but it would do. She couldn't help but smile when she thought of her best friend turned lover. It seemed that after declaring their love for each other last week, everything was falling in place.

They'd decided not to make any definite plans for their future until after Riley and Alpha's wedding. The entire Westmoreland family was excited about the upcoming wedding and expected many of their cousins from out of town to begin arriving this weekend. She had met most of them at one time or another, and she looked forward to seeing them again.

As soon as she sat back down at her desk her cell phone rang and she felt giddy all over when she saw the caller was Stern. He and Canyon had left two days ago for Miami to finalize a deal, and they weren't expected back until sometime tomorrow morning.

She clicked on her phone. "Hello."

"Hello, beautiful."

She smiled. "You wouldn't call me that if you could see me. I'm still at the shop."

"The shop? Why so late?"

"Reports. I have to keep the government happy. I miss you."

"I miss you, too. But guess what."

"What?"

"Canyon and I finalized everything and decided to return home early."

She sat up straight. "How early?"

She could hear his chuckle. "Tonight. Our plane just landed."

"You're back in Denver?" she asked, unable to contain her excitement.

"Yes. Canyon has gone to get the car. I was going to have him drop me off at your place, but you won't be there."

Already she was placing the papers on her desk in a stack. "Wanna bet? I'm leaving now so I'll make it home before you do."

"Um, I don't want to come between you and Uncle Sam."

"I'll finish the reports tomorrow." Just then she heard a crash. "Hold on, Stern. I think I heard something," she said, getting up from her desk.

"Wait! You're there alone?"

"Yes."

"Then stay put and call the police."

JoJo rolled her eyes. "Stern, I can handle—"

"I know you can, but humor me. Canyon just pulled up and we're headed there. We're less than ten minutes away."

JoJo let out an exasperated sigh. Only if they flew. "The alarm is on. It's probably nothing but a stray cat that somehow got locked up inside. It's happened before."

"I know, but I prefer being the one to check it out to make sure. Is your office door locked?"

"No."

"Then lock it and stay put."

Rolling her eyes, she left her seat to go lock the door just as the door crashed open.

"Walter!"

Walter?

Stern went still. He'd clearly heard the name she'd called out but now all he heard was muffled voices. Then her phone went dead. "JoJo? What's going on? You still there?"

When he didn't get a response, he punched in the emergency number. An operator picked up immediately. "I'd like to report a break-in at the Golden Wrench Auto Repair Shop. I was talking to the owner when a man named Walter Carmichael burst into her office. Carmichael has a history of harassing women."

Chills went up Stern's spine when he remembered what sounded like JoJo's door bursting open. "This is Stern Westmoreland," he said when the operator asked that he identify himself.

After hanging up the phone, he glanced over at Canyon, who was driving. Canyon caught his eye and then pressed his foot on the gas and sped down the interstate.

"I heard. We're on our way," Canyon said. "I just hope we get to the shop before JoJo takes the man apart. Evidently, he doesn't know who he's dealing with."

Anger consumed Stern. "Evidently."

"Take your filthy hands off me, Walter."

"Not until I'm good and ready. And you have a lot of nerve calling me filthy, grease lady."

JoJo drew in a deep breath, trying to control her anger. Otherwise, she would break every bone in his body. She still might. She had been so shocked at seeing him that she hadn't had time to defend herself. He'd quickly dived at her and grabbed her, knocking her hard against the desk and sending her cell phone flying to the floor. She wondered if Stern was still on the line. Had he heard anything? Was he calling the police?

"Why are you here, Walter? What do you want?"

"I warned you that I would make you pay for being a tease. You owe me a night and I'm getting it. It doesn't matter to me if I have to take it."

She'd like to see him try. Did he really think he would force himself on her and get away with it? "You're willing to risk your reputation, your job, your—"

"My old man will handle you like he did all the others."

JoJo swallowed. "What others?"

"All those women who tried bringing charges against me, as if they didn't enjoy what I did to them. But Dad proved they all had a price, which I'm sure you do, too. My old man will pay up. He always does, to keep things quiet." Walter then made the mistake of shoving her away from him before shouting, "Now take off your clothes!"

Now he'd really made her mad. Thinking about those other women, who had been at his mercy, and his father, who had bought them off, really had her blood boiling. "Take off my clothes? For you? Don't hold your breath," she snarled.

She saw anger flash in his eyes. He seemed furious that she had the nerve to refuse him. Intense anger distorted his face as he moved toward her. "No problem, I'll take them off myself."

She noticed he didn't have any kind of weapon. Apparently he assumed he could handle her with his bare hands. "Stop, Walter!" she said, issuing her warning. "I don't want to hurt you."

He laughed hard. "You can't hurt me, but I intend to hurt you."

He lunged for her.

Canyon, Stern and a patrol car arrived at the Golden Wrench at the same time and everyone was out of their cars in a flash. Stern saw one of the officers was Deputy Pete Higgins, Derringer's best friend. They were racing toward the front of the building when they heard a chilling scream…from a man.

Canyon glanced over at Stern and a wry smile touched his lips. "Sounds like we're too late."

"The bastard got what was coming to him," Stern said angrily.

The lock on the entry door had been jimmied. With guns drawn, the two officers cautiously made their way inside the building. Ignoring the officers' orders to stay back, Canyon and Stern were right behind them.

The door to JoJo's office was wide-open, barely hanging on by the hinges. When they walked inside they found Walter Carmichael in the middle of the floor, holding his crotch and sobbing like a baby. A cool, calm and collected JoJo sat behind her desk working on her reports.

She glanced up at them and smiled sweetly. "I stayed put just like Stern told me to do."

More patrolmen arrived on the scene, reports were taken and Walter would be taken to the emergency room. While he lay on the stretcher, still sobbing, Stern walked over to him.

"Didn't you know that besides being a black-belt champ JoJo's also a marksman? You're lucky she didn't shoot you. She's also a skilled archer. Can you imagine how it would feel if she'd used a bow and arrow?"

Stern paused to let his words sink in before saying, "You're going to jail for what you tried to do. Just in case your old man's money gets you off, I suggest you not come back this way. JoJo holds grudges."

When Stern saw stark fear in the man's eyes, he couldn't help but chuckle before walking off to where JoJo was giving a final report to Pete.

"Can I take her home now?" Stern asked.

"In a minute," Pete said, frowning. "I'm trying to figure out how Carmichael got past your alarm system."

"My new guy," JoJo said. "Walter bragged about paying my new guy, Maceo Armstrong, money to report whenever I'm here working late. And he paid extra to have Maceo cut a wire in the alarm system."

Pete nodded. "You got Armstrong's address?"

"Yes. It's on file in my office."

"Good. We're going to pick him up."

An hour later, Stern and JoJo were at her place. She

was in the shower and Stern was in the kitchen pouring glasses of wine. He entered the bedroom just as she walked out of the bathroom wearing a velour bathrobe.

"Here, you need this," he said, handing her a glass of wine. "You deserve it."

She took a sip and smiled at him. "Mmm, delicious." She then sat down on the edge of the bed. "Walter got just what he deserved, you know."

Stern chuckled. "You'll never be able to convince him of that. It was pathetic to hear a grown man cry."

She shrugged. "Like I said, he deserved it. The nerve of him, thinking he could rape me without me doing anything about it."

"He might not be able to walk again," Stern said, smiling, liking the idea. "Or have sex," he added, liking that idea even better. He paused and took a sip of his wine. "I hope I never make you mad."

"You can handle me."

Stern thought about what she'd said. Yes, he could handle her, but after a night like tonight, he was glad she could also handle herself. "I propose a toast," he said, lifting up his wineglass.

"To what?"

"To whom. Your daddy, who had the insight to raise a daughter who could take care of herself."

JoJo thought about what he'd said and got kind of misty-eyed. She held up her glass and clinked it against his.

"And to you, Stern. For being a man who knows me, inside and out, and who loves me anyway. And for being a man who lets me know it's okay to be myself and ask for what I want. That means a lot."

After taking a sip of wine, she placed her glass on the

table beside the bed, stood and pushed her robe off her shoulders. "I think you know what I want now."

Yes, he knew.

Stern pulled her into his arms and kissed her hard and deep.

Epilogue

Tucking her hand into Stern's, JoJo sat beside him in the packed church as everyone watched Riley and Alpha join their lives together as man and wife. It was a beautiful ceremony and, not surprisingly, the bride, who was an event planner, had arranged the entire thing with help from the Westmoreland women. It had truly been a storybook wedding. The groom was devastatingly handsome and the bride was outrageously beautiful.

When JoJo had woken up that morning to an empty bed, she'd later found Stern standing outside on her patio staring up at the sky and drinking coffee. She'd tightened her robe around her before opening the French doors to step outside and join him.

He'd turned when he saw her and smiled.

"You okay?" she asked him.

This was the last weekend in September and the weather was turning colder. The wind blowing off the mountains was brisk.

"Yes. I was thinking about just how blessed the Westmorelands are, especially the men. They have been lucky to find women who complement them, women worthy of loving forever. I see my brothers and how happy they are with their wives and families, but I never entertained the thought of finding a woman to share that same happiness with me. Now I know why."

She glanced up at him. "Why?"

"Because I had that woman by my side all along. You were my best friend and the woman destined to be a part of my life forever, as my soul mate, my wife…the mother of my children."

Tears stung JoJo's eyes. "What are you saying, Stern?"

He turned to her and smoothed her hair back from her face. "That I love you and want to marry you. I want you to share my name and be with me always. Will you marry me, JoJo?"

She smiled through her tears. "Yes! Yes! I'll marry you."

Loud clapping intruded into JoJo's thoughts and brought her back to the present. The minister had just presented Riley and Alpha as man and wife and everyone was on their feet, clapping and cheering. Riley swept his bride into his arms and walked out of the church. It had been a beautiful wedding and now it was time to leave for the reception.

Still holding her hand, Stern led her outside where they joined Canyon and his wife, Keisha, and their son, Beau, along with Zane and his fiancée, Channing. Zane and Channing would be tying the knot around the holidays, so another Westmoreland wedding would be taking place in a few months.

JoJo and Stern hadn't yet announced their engagement to anyone, preferring to let Riley and Alpha enjoy their day without any new family news.

Stern leaned down and kissed her on the cheek. "What was that for?" she asked.

"Being you."

"Oh." She leaned up on tiptoe and returned the favor.

"And what was that for?" he asked her.

She gave him a bright smile. "For not just seeing me on the outside but appreciating the inside, too."

He leaned down and whispered sexily, "And I do enjoy the inside."

She was sure her cheeks darkened.

"Come on," he said, tightening her hand in his. "Let's go talk to my cousins from Atlanta who are chatting with Dillon and Ramsey. I think I'll ask Thorn to build us a couple of bikes."

JoJo liked the idea. "Okay. Who is that young woman with Thorn and his wife, Tara?"

"That's Tara sister. She might be relocating to the area from Florida, and Thorn and Tara wanted her to meet all of us."

JoJo nodded. "She's very pretty."

"Come on, let me introduce you," Stern said.

"All right."

As they walked toward the group, for some reason, the thought of Walter Carmichael crossed her mind. He was still in jail awaiting trial. Unfortunately, the Carmichael family had suffered a major setback when the judge had denied bail. Even Walter's father's money hadn't helped him. JoJo believed Walter had a mental illness and she hoped he would get the help he needed.

Maceo Armstrong had gotten into trouble for assisting Walter. And then the young man had gone on to confess that he had been the reason for all her missing inventory. He had been stealing auto parts from her and selling them. She had liked him and had been very disappointed in his duplicity.

Before they reached the group of cousins, Stern stopped walking, pulled her into his arms and spun her around. "You're beautiful and I love you," he said, placing her back on her feet.

She laughed, catching her breath. "And I love you, too."

He leaned down and said, "I have plans for you later."

She smiled up at him, the man who held her heart. "And I definitely have plans for you."

* * * * *

Don't miss Aiden's and Adrian's stories,
coming soon!
Only from Brenda Jackson and Harlequin Desire!